He's the New Generation of Royals.

At fifteen, Prince William is almost as tall as his 5'10" mother . . . he's known for giving his body-guards the slip . . . he's a talented artist like his father . . . he has hung out with Cindy Crawford (and has a pinup of *Baywatch* babe Pamela Lee in his locker at Eton) . . . and he loves the band Pulp (and even got an autographed poster the old-fashioned way, by writing them a fan letter).

Meet Prince William, the hottest new heartthrob on the British teen scene. Learn all about his life at Eton College; his relationship with his mother, Princess Di (the most photographed woman in the world), and his father, Charles (the man who will be king); his brother, Harry, and his cousins Beatrice and Eugenie (the daughters of Prince Andrew and Fergie); his cool vacations, his social life, his crushes, who he's dated so far—and what it's *really* like to be the girlfriend of Prince Charming. *Everything* you've always wanted to know about . . .

Prince William

Books by Randi Reisfeld

Clueless
  An American Betty in Paris
  Cher's Furiously Fit Workout
  Cher Goes Enviro-Mental
  Too Hottie to Handle
Melrose Place: Meet the Stars of the Hottest New TV Show
Joey Lawrence
Prince William: The Boy Who Will Be King

Available from ARCHWAY Paperbacks

For orders other than by individual consumers, Pocket Books grants a discount on the purchase of **10 or more** copies of single titles for special markets or premium use. For further details, please write to the Vice-President of Special Markets, Pocket Books, 1633 Broadway, New York, NY 10019-6785, 8th Floor.

For information on how individual consumers can place orders, please write to Mail Order Department, Simon & Schuster Inc., 200 Old Tappan Road, Old Tappan, NJ 07675.

PRINCE WILLIAM

THE BOY WHO WILL BE KING

AN UNAUTHORIZED BIOGRAPHY

RANDI REISFELD

AN ARCHWAY PAPERBACK
Published by POCKET BOOKS
New York London Toronto Sydney Tokyo Singapore

The sale of this book without its cover is unauthorized. If you purchased this book without a cover, you should be aware that it was reported to the publisher as "unsold and destroyed." Neither the author nor the publisher has received payment for the sale of this "stripped book."

AN ARCHWAY PAPERBACK *Original*

 An Archway Paperback published by
POCKET BOOKS, a division of Simon & Schuster Inc.
1230 Avenue of the Americas, New York, NY 10020

Copyright © 1997 by Randi Reisfeld

All rights reserved, including the right to reproduce this book or portions thereof in any form whatsoever. For information address Pocket Books, 1230 Avenue of the Americas, New York, NY 10020

ISBN: 0-671-88785-8

First Archway Paperback printing June 1997

10 9 8 7 6 5 4 3

AN ARCHWAY PAPERBACK and colophon are registered trademarks of Simon & Schuster Inc.

Cover photo by Alpha/Globe Photos, Inc.

Printed in the U.S.A.

IL 4+

Acknowledgments

The author gratefully acknowledges Lisa Clancy of Archway Paperbacks, who came up with the idea; and Stacey Woolf for her valuable contributions.

To Janet Macoska, John and Winnie Awarski, Leo Schenker, Sharon and Ilan: jolly good job on the research, info and updates: thanks!! For the support and snacks: love to Marvin, Scott, Stefanie and Peabo.

Contents

Introduction

William Windsor is fifteen, tall, handsome, athletic, and rich. He's the hottest new heartthrob on the British teen scene and is rapidly capturing the imaginations of American and Canadian teenagers as well. Magazine articles, pinups, posters, and stickers featuring "Wills," as he's affectionately called, have saturated the newsstands, eagerly snapped up by fans across the globe. A Wills sighting, by photographer, journalist, or fan, is considered a major event.

Wills is not a rock star, nor a movie star, a sitcom icon, or even an Olympic phenom. In fact, the fair-haired lad hasn't done one single thing that might account for his overwhelming popularity—except be born, that is.

But that, after all, was all he had to do. For Wills, more formally known as Prince William, was to the spotlight born, and will to the spotlight always be drawn—even if sometimes, it seems, he's kicking and screaming all the way. William Arthur Philip Louis Windsor is the grandson of Britain's Queen Elizabeth II. He is the firstborn of Prince Charles and Princess Diana, perhaps the most famous and certainly most photographed pair in the world. Their courtship, marriage, and subsequent scandals, battles, and finally, divorce, have been headline news all over the world for nearly two decades. But Wills's fame is only partly due to royal family feuds; he has his own claim as well. Prince William is heir to the British crown: That is, someday he will rule Britain as King William V.

When "someday" will come is anyone's guess, but for Wills it couldn't be late enough. Unlike another future (albeit fictional) monarch, *The Lion King*'s Simba, Wills *can,* very much, wait to be king: He reportedly said he'd just as soon never be crowned.

For now, Wills has his hands full just trying to be a normal teenager, making friends, studying for exams, listening to rock music, going to dances, going on dates, and dealing with his divorced parents. Imagine having it all—every word, every step, every accomplishment, goof, embarrassment, and failure—reported on and gossiped about the world over. Wills doesn't have to imagine what that's like: that *is* his life. What's more, he knows it will always be his life.

That, and one more thing: It isn't only the eyes of the world that are upon him; young Wills also bears the hopes of a nation on his still-growing shoulders. For England's monarchy, a centuries old and deeply revered tradition, may be in serious jeopardy. Some say Wills is the only person who can save it!

Just like Simba, Wills has learned an irrefutable truth: Being a royal heir can be a royal pain. How is Wills dealing with it? Well, it takes more than a few bars of "Hakuna Matata," that's for sure. But Wills has something better than a mere "problem free philosophy," something very pure and very powerful. This is his innate intelligence and true warmth, a vast reserve of inner strength, and the devout adoration of his country. People love Wills and that love can take him far.

But what kind of teen is Wills? What's he *really* like? How much might an ordinary teen have in common with him? What are an ordinary girl's chances of dating him? What is it about him that inspires such devotion and adoration among the world's teens—some of whom will someday be his royal subjects? Learn it all: The amazing life story of Prince William begins now!

PRINCE WILLIAM

THE BOY WHO WILL BE KING

Chapter One

Birth and Circumstance

*I*t is a brisk, breezy, and brightly sunny autumn afternoon in Eton, England, a small town abutting the Thames River. Three good-looking teenage boys, students at the famous school that occupies most of the town, are walking slowly down a narrow, cobblestone street. Two have close-cropped dark hair, the third, who is walking between them, is wearing a baseball cap. Peeking out from beneath its rim, wisps of blond hair are visible. Except for the cap, all three are otherwise dressed similarly, that is, not unlike teenage boys all over the Western world. Their pants are khakis, their shirts, the long-sleeved button-down type that may have come from Benetton or The Gap; their sneakers bear an instantly recognizable brand-name logo. Woolen jackets, albeit unbuttoned, protect them from the afternoon chill.

Their conversation is as commonplace as their look. There's talk of the new album by the rock group Pulp, the surprise questions on this morning's history quiz, the fortunes of their school's soccer team, and a bit about a girl one of them would like to ask out. All are massively hungry and, in fact, on their way to a fast-food joint for a snack.

What could be a more normal scenario on a bright, sunny afternoon such as this one? A better question is: What could be less normal?

The main clue that something about this scene is not quite as ordinary as it appears are the two scrupulously alert adults who are walking a few paces behind the boys. These men are neither talking nor appreciating the fine fall afternoon. They're working at a job they take very seriously. Although they're dressed in plain clothes, both are high-level detectives straight out of Scotland Yard, London's most elite police force. Neither takes his eyes off the boys, not even for one second. When the teens turn a corner, the men carefully follow. But the boys are not suspected of any wrongdoing. They're not about to be cuffed or collared by the cops. In fact, the officers are more or less employed by one of them, or on behalf of him—the one in the middle, that is, the blond with the baseball cap.

For all appearances to the contrary, he is no ordinary boy, much as he might sometimes wish to be. He is very famous, so famous that he needs round-the-clock protection; so famous that an ordinary freedom like taking a kick-back afternoon stroll with his buddies requires surveillance. His is the kind of fame that is not fleeting. That adage "everyone will be famous for fifteen minutes" just does not apply to him. His fame will last his entire lifetime and beyond. Certainly, it started way before his birth.

His friends call him William. The school roster lists him as William Windsor. To the rest of the world, however, he is England's Prince William. And one day he'll be known by another name, King William V.

For the foreseeable future, however, he's Prince William. He is fifteen years old, and like a lot of boys his age, he's into rock music, movies, sports, hanging out with his friends, and girls. Unlike most boys his age, however, he not only knows what his career will be, he's been in training for it since birth. *Career,* perhaps, is too mild a word, for Prince William has a date with destiny, and it is a daunting one.

This is his story.

The day Prince William was born, June 21, 1982, was a national day of rejoicing in Great Britain. It was Monday, the first day of summer that year, and all over the British Isles, celebrations commenced. From the bustling boulevards of cities like London and Liverpool to the quaint countryside of the Cotswolds, to seaside towns and provinces, people partied hearty, with the hearty approval of their bosses and authorities throughout the land.

What exactly was the big deal? A child had come into the world, much like millions do daily. Few inspire *this* kind of widespread rejoicing. This child did, however, not because he was any kind of miracle baby, or the circumstances surrounding his birth were unusual, but simply because just by being born, his place in world history was sealed. In other words, his birth, and much of his life, would be chronicled in all school textbooks dealing with British history.

William was born into the most special kind of royalty—the kind that automatically ascends to the throne. He has neither to be brilliant nor particularly accomplished, wise, or even nice. Because he's a boy, his birthright is secure. Though it might change someday, the tradition of the British monarchy has always been that the firstborn son of the ruling king or queen is automatically next in line for the throne, canceling out any sisters who may have been born before him. Only if there are no male heirs to the ruling monarch, the women in the family ascend. Such has been the case for the past forty-five years, since Queen Elizabeth II has been on the throne. The title of the future king of England is always the same: the Prince of Wales.

Queen Elizabeth is the current ruling monarch, much revered and respected, and by some accounts, the richest woman in the world. She is also William's grandmother. His father, Prince Charles, is Elizabeth's firstborn son. Which means, according to tradition, Charles will be king next—and then it's William's turn. But it wasn't just William's genealogy and destiny that inspired such mass hoopla on the day of his birth. It was also symbolic of how the people of England felt about William's parents.

At the time His Royal Highness Prince Charles and Her Royal Highness Princess Diana were much more than Britain's reigning heirs. They were like a royal super-couple, beloved and besieged with love the world over. Their courtship, wedding, and marriage was very much like a fairy tale, and William's birth was very much a part of the "happily ever after."

To understand William's life, to really get to know him, and see why he has captured the imagination, hearts, and hopes of his country, it helps to know a little about his parents.

William's father, whose full name is Charles Philip Arthur George Mountbatten, was born on November 14, 1948, to Princess Elizabeth and her husband, Prince Philip Mountbatten, the Duke of Edinburgh. When Charles was three, his grandfather, King George VI, died. Since George was Elizabeth's father, and there were no brothers, she then became Queen of England.

Like William, young Charles was destined to be king from the start, but his upbringing was very different from the one planned for his son. Charles was born not at a hospital, but at home, at the official London residence of the queen, Buckingham Palace. That was the tradition back then. In fact, Prince Charles was bound by many traditions. No matter what his personality, strengths, or weaknesses, he was expected to be athletic, outgoing, and musically inclined. However, according to published reports, as a child, Charles was none of the above. Instead, he was naturally shy, very nervous, and far from a natural athlete. In time, however, and with lots of coaching, he learned to be all of the above. By his early adulthood, he'd mastered piano, become quite comfortable with crowds, and was an able sportsman. Skiing, hunting, polo, and sailing are only a few of his avid pursuits.

Like future monarchs before him, Charles—who had a younger sister, Princess Anne, and two much younger brothers, Princes Andrew and Edward—was brought up mostly by stern nannies and at first educated at home by tutors. Later, he was sent away to various and exclusive prep schools. His early encounters with the outside world were intimidating. Young Charles had not been at Cheam prep school for three months when over sixty-eight newspaper and magazine stories about him came out. Schoolmates and others who came into contact with him were easily bribed by the press to tell tales about him. Charles could never feel secure that others wanted to be his friend just because they liked him—but rather, for what they could score off him. The situation was much the same at his next school, the rigorous Gordonstoun in Scotland.

Eventually, Charles managed to cope with his unique situation and make the best of his station in life. He went on to the university, and then, as royals traditionally do, the navy. He stepped into his role as king-in-waiting with aplomb. Still, he never forgot his early childhood experiences. Charles has publicly admitted that they not only scarred him for life, they made him determined that any children he might have would not suffer the same embarrassments. Not if he could help it, anyway.

William's mother, Princess Diana, also had a difficult childhood. And much like Charles, it also made her determined that her future children would be brought up differently. Of course, Diana had no clue that her future children would be the leaders of her country one day. But it wasn't completely outside the realm of possibility, either. For Diana Spencer also came from royal lineage.

Diana was the third daughter of John Althorp, whose royal title became the eighth Earl of Spencer. He was descended from a long line of earls, lords, and viscounts. Her mother was Frances Ruth Burke Roche, who also boasted a royal heritage. Diana was born on July 1, 1961. The Althorps were titled and well-off, and very well-acquainted with the royal family. Both of Diana's grandmothers were at different times ladies-in-waiting (a companion and/or personal assistant) to the Queen Mum, who was married to King George VI and is Queen Elizabeth's mother. Diana's grandfather was a close personal friend of King George VI. The men played tennis together.

Because of their ties to the ruling family, the Althorps were granted a lease of a ten-bedroom home on Sandringham, the queen's country estate in Norfolk. It was called Park House, and Diana, her older sisters Sarah and Jane, and her younger brother Charles, all were born there. They were all, as upper-class British children often are, attended by nannies and educated mostly in private boarding schools. Diana also went, for a year, to a Swiss "finishing" school, a private girls school that stresses training in cultural subjects and social activities.

Diana may have had riches, but she probably would have traded them for a happy family life. When she was six years old, her parents separated and her mother moved away to London. Diana, Sarah, Jane, and Charles remained with their father at Park House, but for the next two years she and her siblings were the subjects of a nasty and very public custody battle. Diana got an early taste of what it was like to be taunted by schoolmates and the object of gossip. It left a bitter taste.

In time, however, the family strife eased up and the custody battle was settled. It was Diana's father who got custody, partly because he was the titled parent. That began a period where Diana shuffled between her parents, spending some time with her mom and new stepfather, Peter Shand Kydd, in London and some with her father in Norfolk. By most accounts, Diana was able to remain on good terms with both parents.

When Diana was fourteen, her grandfather died, and her father assumed his royal title of the eighth Earl of Spencer and moved with the children to the Althorp family's estate in Northamptonshire. At that point Diana officially became Lady Diana Spencer. As she grew, she flourished and gained a reputation for loving fashion, parties, and dances, and making friends easily.

One who couldn't exactly be called a friend right off, however, was Prince Charles.

Diana and her future husband first met, almost in passing, when she was eight years old during a holiday celebration at Sandringham. He was twenty-one. They next came into contact when she was sixteen, he, twenty-nine. Charles was dating her sister, Sarah, and so had come to Althorp house. Diana was a friend of Charles's younger brothers, Andrew and Edward, who were closer to her own age. Still, Charles noticed that Diana had grown up and was quite lovely.

Over the next few years, Charles was starting to be pressured, by his parents *and* by his countrymen, to get married. The heir to the throne was, after all, in his mid-thirties and still had not settled on the proper woman to marry. Of course, a future king couldn't choose just anyone. The woman he selected had to meet many requirements; after all, she'd one day be Queen of England. By tradition, she had to be of either titled or royal lineage; she was supposed to be free of (any sort of) scandal, never before married, not a Roman Catholic, and preferably someone who could handle the pressures and publicity of the "job." Not least of all, Charles's future intended had to have the stamp of approval of his mother, the queen. As for love? Charles himself said, "[Marriage is] the last decision where I would want my heart to rule my head." Love, in effect, would be a bonus to a suitable match, but not the guiding force. That may seem sad but, up until recently, was a stark reality of being a British monarch. It may very well be the same reality William faces in the future.

In 1979 Charles's brother Andrew invited the then eighteen-year-old Diana to spend the summer holidays with his family at their vacation estate in Balmoral, Scotland. By most accounts, that is when Diana fell in love with Charles, and he, for all appearances, with her. Serendipitously, Diana met all the requirements for a royal match. She was titled—Lady Diana Spencer at that point—familiar with the royal world, innocent of scandal, beautiful, guileless, and kind. The thirteen-year age difference between Charles and Diana was not considered a problem. At the time she and Charles starting dating seriously, Diana, who did not go to college, was a teaching assistant at a kindergarten. She loved children.

It didn't take long for all of Britain, and then the rest of the world, to fall in love with her. Soon after Prince Charles proposed, Diana got a taste of the upside *and* the downside of being a future queen. The public went crazy for her; so did the press, who "ambushed" her at work, at home, anywhere to get a shot. Diana might have been unused to the spotlight, but she was a quick study. She learned to take the "inquiring minds" and the shutterbugs in stride. A good thing, too: One day she'd earn the dubious achievement of being the most photographed woman in the world.

The wedding of Charles and Diana, on July 29, 1981, was declared a national holiday in Britain. It played out like a perfect fairy tale, complete with a handsome, besotted bridegroom in full military uniform and, of course, a beautiful blushing bride in an exquisite wedding dress with a yards-long train. The ceremony even included the part where the beautiful princess climbs into a glass coach and is driven through the streets of the kingdom, until she reached her destination, St. Paul's Cathedral. There, her bridegroom awaited. "The wedding of the century," as it was called, was witnessed by hundreds of thousands in the streets; an astounding 750 million people worldwide watched it live on TV. After the couple, now officially His Royal Highness The Prince of Wales, and Her Royal Highness The Princess of Wales, said their "I do's," there was nary a dry eye in the chapel. Even Prince Charles was so moved as to say, "I expect to spend the rest of the day in tears."

After their honeymoon Charles and Diana settled into two official residences, one in London called Kensington Palace and a country place in Gloucestershire called Highgrove. They also spent much time at the royal family's Scottish abode, Balmoral, which has always been a favorite of Prince Charles's.

Perhaps the only event more joyous than the wedding itself was the announcement, several months later, that the happy couple was expecting an heir. That declaration set off a flurry of activity, as all of England waited in joyous anticipation for the birth of their own fairy-tale couple's first child.

Chapter Two

The World's Most
Famous Baby

Unlike his father, Prince William wasn't born at home but in a hospital. While he wasn't the first royal to come into the world in a modern medical facility, the tradition only dates back to 1970. But once a new tradition is begun, it's generally followed. In 1974 the St. Mary's Hospital in the Paddington section of London was chosen as the site of future royal births, and that is where at five A.M. the morning of June 21, 1982, Princess Diana was ferried to await the blessed event. She was met there by the queen's own surgeon gynecologist, Mr. George Pinker, who would deliver the baby.

William was welcomed into the world by crowds numbering in the hundreds of thousands. For as soon as news leaked out that the birth was imminent, throngs of people gathered by the hospital. Other crowds congregated outside all the royal residences—at Buckingham Palace, where the queen resides, and around such estates as Windsor, Highgrove, Sandringham, and Balmoral.

Spirits were high with anticipation throughout England, all the British Isles (Scotland, Ireland, and Wales), and the Commonwealth—which comprises the United Kingdom, its dependencies, and many former British colonies that are now sovereign states (such as Australia, New Zealand, and Canada); they all share a common allegiance to the British Crown.

Much later that night the wait was over. While most people send out birth announcements to family and friends, William's went out to the entire world. That's because, from the get-go, William was everybody's baby. He belonged not only to his family, but to all of Great Britain, and as such, all of Great Britain hung on to his every first, his every accomplishment, every move.

His birth announcement was posted on a gilded easel outside the gates of Buckingham Palace. It was succinct: "The Princess of Wales was safely delivered of a son at 9:03 P.M. today. Her Royal Highness and her child are doing well."

There was no mention of a name in the announcement, because one (or several!) had yet to be chosen. While there was no mention of the baby's birth weight, it later was revealed that the new infant weighed seven pounds, one and a half ounces, had blue eyes and fair hair, and "cried lustily." The crowds went wild, singing, cheering, and applauding the country's new heir. One town near Charles and Diana's country home decorated all the streets with bunting.

At 11 P.M. that same night His Royal Highness Prince Charles made an appearance outside the hospital and told the crowds that the new baby was "beautiful and in marvelous form." What he didn't say, because he probably didn't know just then, was that the newborn and Princess Diana wouldn't be staying at the hospital very long. Within twenty-four hours of his birth, the infant heir went home with his parents. That afforded the nation its first peek at their future leader. All wrapped up in a soft white baby blanket, William lay in his mother's arms as photographers snapped away. Of course, at twenty-four hours old, he was completely unaware of any sort of hoopla, but being photographed, wondered about, and held in awe is William's lot in life. It started immediately!

In fact, the day after his birth, June 22, saw celebrations throughout the nation. The King's Troop, the Royal Horse Artillery, rode in full dress uniform from their barracks at St. John's Wood to Hyde Park to fire a forty-one-gun salute in honor of the infant prince. At the same time the Honorable Artillery Company fired a similar number of salvoes by the Tower of London. Bells rang out from Westminster Abbey from 12 noon to 1:30; and later, from St. Paul's Cathedral, as well as from many other churches around the country. The news was broadcast all over the world, and soon flowers and tributes came flooding in.

It isn't unusual that the birth of a future king be celebrated so grandly, but there was even more joy than perhaps normal at Prince William's entry into the world. A healthy child meant an automatic continuation of the revered monarchy; a healthy boy meant even more. It was the first time since 1910 that there had been two males, father and son, in direct succession to the throne. Clearly, a lot was resting on William's infant shoulders from the get-go.

While the royal baby had the adoration of a nation, what he didn't have in his first few days of life was a name! Partly that's because the naming of a future king is not a matter undertaken lightly. His name will be forever recorded in world history books and is bound by some tradition, which includes mixing the old with the new; combining history with sentiment. But he remained nameless for a while also because his parents couldn't agree. Reportedly, Charles wanted Arthur. Diana lobbied for William, which means "will" and "helmet," and was a common name of English and Scottish kings in past centuries. The last British king of that name was William IV, who ruled 1830–37.

A compromise was reached, but it wasn't until several weeks after his birth that the baby was officially named William Arthur Philip Louis. The second two names, Philip and Louis, were tributes to people in Charles's family, including the baby's own grandfather, Prince Philip. His last name, Windsor, signifies that he is from the House of Windsor monarchy. If he weren't a royal, he would have the same last name as his paternal grandfather, Mountbatten.

William was officially named in a naming ceremony, and that is when his birth certificate was filled out. It lists him officially as "His Royal Highness Prince William Arthur Philip Louis."

Unsurprisingly, a slew of nicknames soon followed. His mom invented Wills—which is the one that's really stuck. His dad dubbed him "Willie Wombat." Over the next few years the press had a field day calling him different "pet" names. One news-inspired nickname came about at the next occasion the media had to cover him: his christening. That's when they dubbed him "The Prince of Wails."

The blessed event of Prince William's christening was held on August 4, 1982—the date was chosen to coincide with the eighty-second birthday of his great-grandmother, the Queen Mum, making for double celebration. It was all steeped in centuries old tradition. It was held in the music room of Buckingham Palace, and William was wrapped in the same royal Victorian christening robe, a gown of Honiton lace, that many of his royal predecessors had worn. It is normally stored at Windsor Castle.

Six esteemed relatives and friends were bestowed the honor of becoming his godparents. They were

Princess Alexandra; ex-King Constantine of Greece (a second cousin and close friend of Charles); Lord Romsey; the Duchess of Westminster; Lady Susan Hussey (a lady-in-waiting to the queen); and Sir Laurens van der Post, an author, mystic, and spiritual guru of Prince Charles's. The christening itself was performed by the Archbishop of Canterbury, the Anglican Church's religious leader.

Baby William acted with princely aplomb through most of the ceremony—until he got hungry, that is. Like any infant, royal or not, a feeling of hunger is primary and will elicit fierce crying until satisfied. Which is exactly what happened at Wills's christening. The twenty-five-minute ceremony itself had ended, but the historic and official photos were yet to be taken. That had to be accomplished before Wills could be fed. Which didn't sit well with the infant, who continued to wail away, thereby earning himself that Prince of Wails nickname. Nothing could stop him, including attempts by his grandparents, who tried to put a light spin on the situation. The elderly Queen Mum praised him for his healthy lungs; the queen herself quipped that this was William's earliest attempt at speechmaking.

Wills's young mother, Diana, finally found a quick solution. She stuck the tip of her pinkie finger in his mouth, giving him something to suck on temporarily while the photos got done. It quieted William, and also created the cutest royal christening photo the world has seen. That and the historic photo of Prince William in the arms of his great-grandmother, the birthday "girl," grabbed front-page space in newspapers and magazines the world over.

If his birth and christening were quite traditional, it didn't mean William's parents had forgotten their own vows about doing things differently with their own children. It started with William's bedroom, or nursery, as it's called. The walls were done in soft pastels, instead of the "hospital green" of the one in Buckingham Palace, where Charles grew up. And instead of being filled with antique cradles and dressers used by his forebears, Wills's room at Kensington Palace was decorated with modern furniture and bright and lively red, white, and blue rabbits.

But William had two "first" homes, and the other, at his parents' country estate in Highgrove, featured an even more elaborate nursery. That one came equipped with a private bathroom and was decorated with murals of fourteen Disney characters—a specially commissioned fantasy that took almost a month to complete. No doubt, it marked the beginning of Wills's fascination with all things Disney.

It's a good thing William had two nurseries, though he would've needed even more to accommodate all the presents he got if he'd kept them. Hundreds upon thousands of gifts came pouring in from all corners of the world. Most went to children's hospitals and orphanages. While there were many from world leaders and other dignitaries, perhaps the most memorable baby gift Wills got was created by lace-makers in a seaside village of England. It was a book of nursery rhymes made entirely in lace—an incredible feat that took ten thousand working hours to accomplish. That gift stayed home!

In the past, children of the monarchy had been brought up primarily by nannies, as their parents were massively occupied with official duties and affairs of state. Although Charles and Diana had vowed to be different—and they were—still, two nannies were hired to care for the infant heir. It was their choice of nanny that surprised traditionalists. For the person they chose, Barbara Barnes, had no official training, except for the on-the-job type. She came highly recommended through friends, which after all, is the way most people would choose an infant caretaker. Like any and all tidbits about Wills, this was duly noted and reported in the papers and debated over. Most praised the choice, as Barbara, as she preferred to be called, became known as a gentle yet firm type, certainly less formal, starchy, and strict than Charles's or Diana's nannies had been. She didn't even wear a uniform. Wills had an "under-nanny," too, named Olga Powell.

No matter how many caregivers were on board, though, Wills's parents tried to spend as much time with him as they could. Like most new parents, they were completely besotted with their baby. Charles, who loved to bathe Wills, wrote a letter to his friend that said, "He really does look surprisingly appetizing and has sausage fingers like mine."

Charles and Diana tried not to be separated from William for any length of time and, to that end, broke a royal tradition when their son was only nine weeks old. They took the baby on the same plane with them for the quick hop from London to Balmoral in Scotland. Normally, royal parents and heirs do not travel in the same plane, but reportedly, Diana insisted on traveling *en famille,* and got her wish.

Prince William's parents also tried hard to protect him from the hot glare of the spotlight. Although the public was insatiable in its desire to see more of the newborn, Charles and Diana were determined not to make a spectacle of him. However, they did understand the country's need for an occasional glimpse of its future king and so set up a schedule of sorts for Wills to be photographed. The plan was that only officially sanctioned photographers would be invited to specially set-up events. The first two had been the day William left the hospital and then the christening.

The next event was when the three-month-old posed for his official portrait. The shot was taken by royal photographer Lord Snowden, who just so happened to be Wills's great-uncle—the husband of his grandmother's sister, Princess Margaret. That first family portrait of Charles, Diana, and a wide-eyed infant William was circulated throughout the world. It eventually showed up on the covers of books about royal babies, on magazine covers, and even on souvenir calendars.

Prince William was next "held" up for public inspection on his first Christmas. He was six months old, and again the shots were taken in a very controlled situation. Selected lensmen were invited to the baby's home at Kensington Palace three days before Christmas. Wills performed like a pro for the cameras, gurgling, chortling, giggling, and sucking on his teething rattle. He spent most of his time staring at the butterflies that decorated a sofa cushion, but when his mom tickled him, he smiled obligingly. When those photos were printed, once again, the little prince charmed an entire nation.

William spent that very first Christmas with his family at Windsor Castle, the weekend residence of the queen. Although he wasn't nearly old enough to appreciate what was going on around him, he did have a very definite and strong personality already. "He earned a reputation for making himself heard" is how one magazine put it—in other words, he cried a lot, and loudly! According to Diana's dad, the six-month-old William also had "an enormous appetite" and was growing accordingly: He weighed seventeen pounds already. He hadn't quite mastered sitting up yet, but he was a pro at *spitting* up—a habit his parents hoped to curb soon. Wills could also crawl and, as his mother said, "snatch at all attractive objects around him." His father, Prince Charles, described baby Wills like this: "He's wonderful fun and really makes you laugh. He's not at all shy. He's a great grinner, but he does dribble a lot."

Because of the security risk, he couldn't be taken for long walks at public parks, so Wills's earliest outdoor experiences were in his pram in the walled-in gardens around Highgrove House and in the private grounds at Kensington Palace. He didn't complain! Prince William's favorite toy at that age was his teddy bear. He was also fascinated with a plastic whale that shot little balls out of the top of its head.

Like most doting grandmothers—even if she is the Queen of England—HRH Elizabeth II carried photos of her adored grandson with her everywhere she went. And like most proud moms, Diana video-taped all her son's infant accomplishments. Back in 1982 the Windsors seemed, for all the world, like an enchanted family; no one knew about any strife, nor were there hints of the discord to come. But much later on it was revealed that Prince William's mom had suffered terrible postpartum depression and developed an eating disorder. She would later say that baby Wills was the only joy in her life.

Diana did not like to be separated from her son for any length of time. Perhaps that's why, when William was only nine months old, he found himself accompanying his parents on a long journey—all the way to Australia and New Zealand. It wasn't a vacation. It was the royal equivalent of a business trip, and taking the baby along was, up until that point, unheard of.

It can be easy to forget that Wills's parents, thrilled with their new baby, still had important obligations. As the reigning Prince and Princess of Wales, part of the job was to participate in "good-will" tours all over the world. In the spring of 1983 they were scheduled for a six-week tour of the Commonwealth country of Australia. Several months before the trip Charles and Diana an-nounced that Wills was coming along. The official word was that the Palace—Wills's grandmother, that is—approved of the plan, in spite of the "hazard of two heirs to the throne traveling together." But off the record, several sources admitted that Diana had to fight her mother-in-law long and hard for the privilege of taking young William. There were other skeptics as well. Some said the only reason Wills was being allowed to come was completely political: that the entire country of Australia would be charmed by the infant heir, and more ready to vote on issues favorable to the continuation of the monarchy.

Whatever the real reason, accompany his parents Wills did—and in doing so, made history for being the first infant heir to the throne to be included on a Royal Tour. He also, unsurprisingly, managed to charm the entire country of Australia, and then New Zealand. Along with his nanny and several other attendants, William actually spent the six weeks in one location, while his parents journeyed throughout the country, coming back to spend each weekend with him. William stayed at a private and isolated country estate, which happened to have a swimming pool. Because the weather was uncommonly warm that spring, a water-winged William took his first dip in a swimming pool. He also got into his first bit of trouble. He dragged a lace tablecloth off a tea table and sent cups and saucers—as well as a plate of biscuits—crashing to the floor.

Naturally, Prince William posed for a carefully controlled photo session with his parents. This time, he demonstrated his ability to crawl, push himself up on his hands, stand up while holding on, chew on a daffodil, and play with a stuffed koala bear toy. He also scooped up a handful of dirt and tried to eat it! His father admitted to the photographers that at this stage in young William's life, his greatest interest was "exploring wastepaper baskets." His mother, unabashedly delighted at her son, was heard to whisper in his ear, "Who's the little superstar, then?"

In this session William was wearing a short-sleeved, one-piece blue romper with white smocking. As soon as the photos appeared in scores of magazines and newspapers around the world, sales of similar baby outfits skyrocketed. In fact, the demand for the same exact outfit was so great that a once-shuttered factory had to be reopened to produce them. In his own way baby William accomplished his first little act of "goodwill" by inadvertently helping to reduce unemployment in his country.

Mass affection for the baby heir, who was next nicknamed "Billy the Kid," skyrocketed as well. Several Australian leaders echoed the thoughts of their constituents by saying to Charles and Diana, "We hope Prince William's presence here will be the first of many visits," and "We look forward to meeting Prince William and getting to know and love him as we love you, sir." Naturally, William's parents were showered with gifts for him on every leg of their trip: fifty thousand were counted before they went home. One particularly memorable offering was a kiwi-feather cloak made by a Maori tribe in New Zealand, a small-scale model of one presented to Prince Charles.

When Wills got back from his thirteen-thousand-mile round-trip sojourn, he enjoyed a well-deserved rest, but his parents had to leave soon after—this time, on a much shorter trip, to another Commonwealth country, Canada. Although the length of the stay was short, they were unfortunately away for William's first birthday. But the event did not go uncelebrated. He woke up to the strains of "Happy Birthday to You," sung by people who'd gathered outside Kensington Palace. Mom and Dad returned with a plane full of gifts from well-wishers all through Canada. There were even more presents waiting back home, including this one: a Shetland pony from the Shetland Pony Stud Society. The horse came with the name "Lion," as well as the expectation that the future king would commence riding lessons sometime around his second birthday.

His parents tried valiantly to strike a balance between the public's constant demand to know every detail of Wills's progress, and to see more of William, and their own desire to keep his life as private as possible. Limited information was dispensed and instantly gobbled up by a hungry public. *Royalty* magazine listed Wills's progress: "He could smile at six weeks; roll onto his tummy and support his upper body on his forearms at seventeen weeks; sit with support at six months, and sit without support shortly afterward. His first tooth peeked out at eight months; he crawled at nine months and took his first steps at ten months, supported by 'Jumbo,' his father's old blue elephant on wheels. He took his first unaided steps at Highgrove and weighed twenty-five pounds at his first birthday."

William's second big "public showing" happened just before his second Christmas, in 1983, when he was eighteen months old. The setting was his own backyard, the gardens at Kensington Palace. The honored guests were photographers and TV news crews. By this time Prince William had grown to a sturdy three feet tall (and boasted eleven teeth). He responded to his parents' urging, "Show them you can walk," by promptly bolting away in the opposite direction of the cameras. He had to be coaxed back into range three times before he cooperated. He wasn't keen on smiling, either, until his mom pointed to her husband and said, "Who's that?" A giant grin spread across Wills's face as he said, "Daddy!" The photographers snapped away, and the results were dozens of happy baby pictures. Wills wore a navy blue snowsuit with the letters ABC embroidered on the front. Sales of those went immediately through the roof!

That public display was one of the first where William, had he been old enough to comprehend, might have felt the double-edged sword of fame. Up until that point, everything written about him was glowing, positive, and positively gushing with goodwill. He was a baby, after all; what could he be criticized for? But as any famous person could have advised him, some segments of the press will always find something negative to say, and so they did about Wills. It was printed that he was "not precocious" (read: not too bright); "slow to crawl" (!), and not cute! "He's rounded and sturdy, but moon-faced and crabby-looking," one report carped. In other words, Wills got dissed for being "unattractive!"

As he grew, word of William's toddler antics spread throughout the land. Soon after learning to walk, he also learned to run—on one memorable occasion, right through an infrared beam that set off a major security scare at Kensington Palace! Another time curious toddler Wills pressed a button—after all, what was it there for if not to be pushed?—and promptly set off the alarm system at Balmoral Castle. He was also fond of climbing into wastebaskets and dropping his father's golf balls into unattended shoes.

An ordinary toddler of William's age would just be starting to have playmates. And although nothing ever was, or will be, ordinary about Prince William, he wasn't without peers. Lucky for him, there were cousins, several around his own age. Wills adored his older cousin Peter Phillips, the son of his aunt, Princess Anne (Charles's sister). It's faint praise that Peter is responsible for teaching Wills to stick out his tongue at the cameras! Wills also enjoyed playing with Peter's sister, Zara, only a year older than himself, and with his cousins on his mother's side, the children of her older sisters Jane and Sarah.

As William's second birthday approached, there was big news on two fronts. First, the little heir had nailed his first important skill: He'd learned to wave to his adoring public. He certainly had no clue why he attracted such large crowds every time he went out, and certainly knew nothing of his daunting destiny. He also had no clue about another big event that would take place in the fall of 1984: the birth of a new baby brother.

Chapter Three

King Tot

The world knew about the impending birth of a sibling for William well before he did. The official announcement was made just before Wills's own second birthday, and as Princess Diana went about her royal rounds, it was clear she was becoming more and more royally round! She was due to give birth to another child in September 1984.

Just as they'd done in anticipation of William's birth, crowds of well-wishers gathered outside St. Mary's Hospital in joyous anticipation of yet another historic and blessed event. They were rewarded on September 15, 1984, when, at 4:40 P.M., Princess Diana gave birth to a six-pound, fourteen-ounce, healthy little boy. This time 'round, the vitally important statistics were made public immediately.

Proud papa Charles, who, it was rumored, had been hoping for a girl, gave his subjects the early scoop: The new baby boy was "marvelous," had pale blue eyes, and indeterminate hair color, which would later be dubbed "rust." This baby got his name a lot more quickly than his older brother had. The day after his birth, it was announced that his official name would be Prince Henry Charles Albert David of Wales, but that he'd be known as Prince Harry.

The press promptly gave him another name, "The Spare." It signified that the British monarchy now had "An Heir and a Spare," a reference to what could happen if the natural heir for some reason did not ascend to the throne. (That situation did occur, much earlier this century, when Edward VIII, the firstborn son of George V, abdicated to marry—for love—someone without royal peerage, known as a commoner. Edward's next-younger brother, George VI, took over: He is Prince William's great-grandfather).

William, just over two years old, came to the hospital the day following his brother's birth. He was Harry's first visitor. Dressed in his Sunday best, red shorts and a white shirt, he looked over in wonder at the crowd of over a thousand gathered outside the hospital. As he walked hand-in-hand with his father up the front steps, William did not give any indication of his feelings about now having a sibling. But he made his feelings evident just a little while later, when he ran to the waiting arms of his mother in her hospital suite. According to published reports, "As William saw his brother, there was a lot of laughter. He was allowed to touch the infant and hold his hand." The visit lasted only fifteen minutes, but it probably helped set the tone for the relationship that would ensue between the two boys. Their father reported that his two sons "got along beautifully, right from the first moment." And from all appearances, Wills's nascent relationship with his baby brother was protective and caring. Later, Charles even said that Wills liked to "get into the cot with the baby and cuddle him."

Once again Princess Diana left the hospital, newborn in tow, very soon after the birth. As they had for Wills, hundreds of thousands of gifts flooded in for Harry. They included white booties that arrived by balloon! The famous singer Barry Manilow sent a five-inch-high antique baby piano. Wills wasn't left out of the gift-giving largesse. Around the time of Harry's birth, possibly to ease the pain of having to share the spotlight and his parents, he was sent a miniature Jaguar sports car, valued at over $100,000. (Later, he'd break it, but that's another story.)

Along with all the well-wishers, there were some naysayers—an occupational hazard when you're so famous that the press reports everything you do. The very day Harry was brought home from the hospital, reports indicated that his father, Prince Charles, did not hang around, but ran off to play polo only an hour after his wife and newest son had settled in. No one was openly suggesting family strife, but looking back, it certainly appears as if the stage was set for what would come later.

It has been written of William's dad that his life was run "by committee," that instead of his parents making decisions on his behalf, entire panels were convened to decide on matters like his education, his instruction in sports and music, even his friendships. It was exactly this sort of upbringing Charles had hated, and did not want for his son. Certainly, Diana, who'd in effect "lost" her mother when she was six, wanted to be as hands-on a parent as she could. And to an extent, they both were. But to a larger extent, they weren't without help, and lots of it. For aside from their nannies, Wills and Harry were attended daily by an entire live-in staff both at Kensington and Highgrove.

There were butlers, secretaries, valets, dressers, cooks, chauffeurs, housekeepers, a cleaning staff, an army orderly as well as numerous aides, all in all a total of about twenty people whose job it was to serve the household and its members. Additionally, Prince William was assigned his own personal detective, a man named Dave Sharp, who functioned as a bodyguard. Wills became instantly attached to his new adult buddy—so much so that his parents feared he was getting too close to one person. In response, they added others to princely detective duty.

Prince William clearly grew up with adults catering to his every whim; that seemed normal to him. But that doesn't mean he necessarily became insolent and bossy. To the contrary, William became friendly with those hired to serve and/or protect him, and that is a trait that continues to this day. He can't help but know he is indeed special, but he also has natural compassion for and unfeigned interest in other people. Both of which, it might be noted, are perfect qualities for the ultimate leadership position he will someday inherit.

No matter how large the staff, the real nurturing of Princes William and Harry was done by their mother. Diana's bedroom was close enough to the nursery so that she could hear an errant whimper in the night. And like most caring moms, she was the one who most often came running if one of the princes cried. Like most normal toddlers, Wills often crawled into bed with her when nightmares frightened him.

Naturally, everything related to the royal toddler was of the greatest interest to all of Britain. Some of that curiosity was satisfied during the scheduled royal photo session when William turned two. For this fifteen-minute "showing," once again in the garden at Kensington Palace, he kicked a soccer ball around (which is called football in England), was pushed on a swing by his dad, and poked his royal head into several camera lenses to see what was inside. Wills didn't reward his public with many smiles, but he did show off his growing vocabulary. He repeated everything his parents said to him. He listened closely to his father, who pointed to the gauntlet of video cameras focused on him and said, "Those are big sausage-things which record everything you say—start learning." Whether or not Wills understood the warning at that tender age is doubtful; he would, however, learn big time, later on.

Between the ages of two and three Wills earned himself a new nickname: King Tot. For not unlike other temper-tossing two-year-olds, he was quite a willful, and sometimes destructive, handful. According to widely published reports, he broke things regularly, attempted to flush his dad's shoes down the toilet and, in general, was "obstreperous and mouthy." His mom tagged him a mini-tornado. One magazine even wrote, "Prince William's publicly recorded trail of destruction is impressive for one so small!" His own father "ratted" him out to the press, admitting that he was "very destructive."

His nanny acknowledged he was "a bit of a handful." Apparently, there was friction between what his softhearted mom would allow him to get away with and what the nanny thought appropriate. There was also, reportedly, a bit of a struggle between Wills's parents over how much influence nanny Barbara had. Charles wanted her to have more; Diana, who did not want her to become a surrogate parent, less. It all led to trouble in nannyland and eventually, Barbara Barnes left "by mutual agreement." A new nanny, Ruth Wallace—whom Harry called Roof, because he couldn't pronounce her name—was then hired. She'd been previously employed by other royals, including Princess Michael of Kent, whose own children were considered the best-mannered of all the royal tots.

Wills had a truly endearing side as well, and it, too, was duly reported on. He was fascinated by the pomp and pageantry of all the army soldiers and officials who lined up, in uniform, to salute his father, Prince Charles. Little Wills delighted in copying the salute whenever his dad walked through the front door.

As Harry grew, he began to imitate Wills, and the sight of the toddler princes saluting Prince Charles was not uncommon in the Windsor household. Nor was, it was being whispered, Charles's more and more frequent absences. While many children grow up with parents who travel frequently on business, few have every minute detail recorded for everyone to read about! But Wills's dad, the direct heir to the throne, was often torn between his royal duties and parental love, an uncomfortable situation to say the least. The year following Harry's birth, Charles's official duties took him to Papua, New Guinea, for a week and on a month-long solo tour to several countries another time.

His dad's absences didn't seem to affect Wills's outgoing disposition, however. Along with his mischievous behavior and fascination with pomp and pageantry, the little boy also seemed to revel in all the attention he was getting. He became more comfortable being photographed. By the age of three Prince William had mastered the art of the handshake—something he'll probably do more of than most people in the entire world. He'd also traveled with his parents on a cruise capping their seventeen-day official tour of Italy; there, he charmed an entire nation and dealt well with the cheering crowds and flashing cameras.

At that age Prince William began to develop a close relationship with his grandmother. Of course, that's not unusual in any family, but for Wills, there is greater significance to that relationship. For the queen of England is the person who would eventually tutor him in royal family history, and in his duties. That part of his serious education would come later, but at the age of three, Wills affectionately called her "Garry," since he couldn't pronounce "Granny," and loved to have her chase him down the red-carpeted corridors of Buckingham Palace! Prince William also learned to swim in the palace pools, with his mom and grandmother close by, encouraging his progress.

On rare quiet days at home when Princess Diana had a break, Wills, munching on his favorite marmite sandwiches (a paste of butterlike consistency, on the spicy side), would often play in her sitting room while she did paperwork. Every once in a while she would stop to do puzzles with him. "He's a very lively normal little boy who does well in all the usual things you would expect a child of that age to do," reported an official from Buckingham Palace, who added that his relationship with Harry continued to be close and loving. Jealousy, if there was any, had not surfaced.

Having his own private pool—in a palace, no less—for swimming lessons is only a small part of the perks and privileges little Wills and his brother Harry grew up with. His two homes, Kensington

Palace and Highgrove, were quite posh. The former
is a redbrick compound on the edge of the 615-acre
Hyde Park in London. It offered a small, walled
garden with plenty of room for Wills and Harry to
wander and kick a soccer ball around, plus a backyard swing set. His family's weekend retreat, Highgrove, was more luxurious still. Located on 1,100
acres in Gloucestershire, 100 miles west of London,
it came equipped with more elaborate gardens, a
private swimming pool, plus six horse stables. In two
of those were quartered Wills's own Shetland pony,
(his second) Trigger, and Harry's, called Smokey.
Wills was assigned a groom, Marian Cox, to teach
him to ride. He took to horseback as easily as he'd
taken to the adulation of the crowds—in 1986, at
the age of four, he was photographed on his pony,
wearing a riding cap and Mickey Mouse T-shirt,
waving gamely for the camera.

The little prince was also privy to sails on the 412-
foot royal yacht *Britannia,* which boasted a crew of
240. Of that number, several were assigned exclu-
sively to him, to keep him out of mischief and, of
course, safely on board. For that purpose, too, Wills
was required to wear a life jacket at all times aboard
the yacht.

There were two helicopters and three aerospace
jets owned by his immediate family. Partly, those
are just perks of being exceedingly wealthy, but there
is a practical side to the glut of luxury vehicles:
Travel comes with the job. William's parents were
expected to maintain a schedule that included a
mind-boggling amount of appointments, official vis-

its, parties, receptions, and charity work, in all sorts
of places. At one point his mom's calendar was
booked up every hour of every day for the following
nine months. During the course of a year, Wills and
his family received fifty thousand invitations!

Another perk of Wills's royal existence is
vacations—and lots of them. Traditionally, the
royals take long, frequent, and spectacular vacations. There's the annual ten-day cruise through the
Western Isles taken every July aboard the royal
yacht. While it allows the family a chance to dress
down and relax, it also provides stops at various
islands for shopping and picnicking on the beach.
Evenings on the yacht, they are entertained by a
string orchestra.

That vacation is followed by a ten-week stay in
Balmoral Castle, which is located on the River Dee
and surrounded by fifty-thousand acres in one of the
most beautiful spots in Scotland. On vacation there,
Prince William enjoyed alfresco picnics with his
family and began his training in such royally sanctioned pursuits as fishing and shooting.

Other royal vacations, including six weeks off
before and during Christmas, plus two weeks at
Easter, were taken in even more glamorous locales,
including the ski slopes of some of the most luxurious places in the world, such as Klosters in Switzerland. When Wills was still a toddler, he traveled to
Spain and spent ten days lying on the beach, cruising
on a private yacht, and relaxing at the summer
palace of that country's King Carlos. Naturally,
Wills continued to accompany his parents on several

of their official travels as well, which made him one exceedingly well-traveled youngster.

No matter how unusual and unusually privileged his life, however, Wills's parents kept up their determination to infuse a sense of normalcy into his childhood. One of the biggest steps in that direction—and away from royal tradition—came in 1985 when Wills was just over three. That was when he started nursery school.

Chapter Four

William the Terrible?

The education of a future king is not taken lightly. In the past, most heirs of Prince William's tender age, including his father, were educated at home, with private tutors. That not only provided one-on-one attention, but also afforded the utmost security. For along with royal perks and privileges also comes the implicit threat (of kidnapping or worse) to the safety and well-being of the little prince.

But Prince Charles and Princess Diana were determined that they could overcome security concerns, so Wills could go to school with his peers. "He is not to miss out on the fun and freedom enjoyed by so many children his age. Above all, he has to be given the opportunity to make his own friends," commented *Royal Monthly Magazine*. An insider

added, "Charles and Diana want William, and later
Harry, to have as normal an existence as possible.
Charles remembers the misery of his own school
years and does not want his children to suffer in the
same way."

At first, that decision did not sit well with the
powers that be at the palace, namely: Her Majesty
the Queen. If Wills were not to be educated at home,
then the queen suggested that a nursery school could
be set up at Kensington Palace, and other children
brought in. There was much heated discussion about
the whole topic, with lists of possible nursery
schools drawn up and thoroughly investigated. Some
were simply too far from home, others deemed
unacceptable because they couldn't provide proper
security. Speculation of where little Wills would be
heading his very first day of school was also taken up
in the press, with lots of ink spent on possible
locales.

In the end, William's parents prevailed over the
queen's wishes. In doing so, they broke with tradition of all previous heirs to the British throne.
September 24, 1985, marked the beginning of
Wills's formal education: his first day at Mrs.
Mynors' Nursery School in a section of West London
called Nottinghill Gate, only ten minutes from
home. The school, housed in a stately brownstone,
sounds ordinary enough, but it did have royal con-
nections: Mrs. Jayne Mynors herself was the sister-
in-law of a cousin to the Queen Mother. A private
school, its price tag was high enough to ensure that

Wills would romp only with similarly privileged tots. And for all the ordinariness it provided him, Prince William came equipped with something—or someone—quite out of the ordinary: his own private armed security guard!

William's first day of school was covered enthusiastically by the media. Hundreds of photographers and reporters were on hand to document the moment when the hesitant but excited three-year-old, wearing a bright red shorts outfit and carrying a Postman Pat lunch box, kissed his parents goodbye and took his first steps through the school's front door. Wills waved to the cameras; a policeman saluted him.

And so William began his life as a "typical" nursery school student. The schoolroom itself was not very different from those of most nursery schools. It was brightly lit and decorated with the letters of the alphabet, numbers, paper balloons, and the students' artwork. Toys, books, and craft supplies filled the shelves and bins. William, as he was called—not (on his parents' instructions) His Royal Highness, or Prince William—even had his very own coatrack set at child-size height. He sat at a foot-high wooden chair and shared a table with six schoolmates.

There were thirty-six children at school with him, divided by age into three groups. Wills started off in the Cygnets group and eventually graduated to the Little Swans and then the Big Swans. His day among his peers consisted of prayers, arts and crafts, and music. In the school's walled-in backyard he played on a slide that was built into a miniature log cabin. For snack breaks Wills brought his own orange drink.

Little has been reported of William's behind-closed-doors behavior at nursery school, but some tidbits have escaped. His best friend was named Nicholas, and together they were somewhat mischievous. Instead of using their paintbrushes on the easel, they'd paint each other's faces. Once, the royal rascal flushed a classmate's lunch down the toilet. None of which would have caused even a ripple if Wills were an ordinary preschooler, but all of which was headline news because ordinary is something he wasn't, nor ever will be.

All told, outgoing Wills had no trouble adjusting to nursery school. His first handmade treasure, a paper mouse, is being kept for posterity. In his two years there, he more than met the goal of the establishment: a happy introduction to school life in general, and a rudimentary knowledge of reading, writing, and arithmetic. Because William was so successful at Mrs. Mynors', his brother Harry followed directly in his footsteps. Unlike his extroverted brother, little Harry seemed quite nervous and withdrawn his first day. Eventually, however, he adapted to it well—except for those occasions when he was compared with William. One reported incident had an irate Harry throwing a mound of clay on the floor when an aide informed him that William was better than he at molding clay.

William's parents' attempts at giving him a normal life did not stop with nursery school. He and his brother (with their bodyguards) were often brought to city playgrounds to frolic among regular kids. They both loved to whoosh down the slides. Unlike previous heirs to the throne, little Prince William got to go to fast-food restaurants like McDonald's for burgers and to amusement parks, where he rode roller coasters and shot the rapids. A favorite destination was the giant slide at Windsor Safari Park.

William didn't have to give up any princely perks for the sake of normalcy. He still had his private riding lessons and expensive vacations aboard yachts. One Christmas the most famous department store in London, Harrods, closed to the public for several hours just so Wills could have it all to himself for Christmas shopping.

In 1986 William was described by his father as "a splendid little character, good-natured—at least he seems to be—he also seems to have quite a good sense of humor and be very outgoing." Perhaps that was a more diplomatic way of saying that Wills was still, by many accounts, a tiny terror.

William attended his first formal family wedding that year. It was the much publicized nuptials of his uncle Prince Andrew (his father's brother) to Sarah Ferguson. While the eyes of the world were upon the royal couple, Wills fidgeted, squirmed, and whispered through the ceremony. Then he picked a fight with a flower girl and made faces at the girls who presented flowers to his grandmother. All of which is behavior not uncommon to any preschooler, but nonetheless newsworthy because of this particular preschooler's pedigree.

In January 1987 Prince William was ready to take the next step in his formal education. As his days at nursery school were coming to an end, William's classmates asked, "Where are you going to school next?" But the young prince couldn't say. "I'm not allowed to know 'cause of security," he reportedly answered. He wanted to go where his friends were headed, and as it turned out, it's extremely possible some did accompany him. For William's next school was practically around the corner from the nursery.

At the time Princess Diana said, "We're open-minded about William and his education. We will find a school that he can adapt to." The one they found, after another intense search, was the Wetherby School, a pre-prep academy for boys only, ages four and a half to eight. Being a day school outside the palace, it continued to represent a break with the royal tradition of at-home education.

The Wetherby School, pricey, small, and structured, was somewhat more formal than Mrs. Mynors' had been. For one thing, Wills, like all the other students, had to wear a uniform of black shorts, a white button-down shirt with red tie, beneath a charcoal-gray jacket embroidered with the school's red crest. A matching brimmed cap completed the school uniform.

William's first day was front-page news. A gathering of reporters withstood the January chill in 1987 to record the event for posterity. Four-and-a-half-year-old William, it was later written, was shy and nervous as he alighted from the car, clutching his mother's legs. But he was poised enough to acknowledge, with a shy smile and a coy wave, the journalists who were calling his name.

The emphasis at Wetherby was not so much rigorous academics but music and manners. In both, William had natural ability. He loved music and listened to it all the time at home, especially his mom's tape of *Phantom of the Opera.* William had already started piano lessons, though the only "tune" he'd mastered so far was "Chopsticks." He also had a head start in the manners department, or so his mom thought. "He opens doors for women and calls men sir," Diana noted with requisite motherly pride.

Despite Wetherby's concentration on music and manners, still it *was* rated one of the top pre-prep schools in London. William joined his class of twenty boys for instruction in reading, writing, arithmetic, geography, plus French, art, and computers. The highlights of the school year were the Christmas Carol Concert and Sports Day, where skills in football (American soccer), cricket, and swimming were demonstrated.

Art was William's favorite subject, and he was quite good at it. But while his schoolmates often drew beach scenes and futuristic cars, William's sketches were usually of castles with yellow splotches in the battlements—to represent "gunfire," he explained. If his fascination with all things military didn't set him apart from his peers, there were enough other signs.

For one, there was the ever-present armed detective on the school grounds every day to watch over William. For another, there was his coatrack. While the other boys simply had their first names to identify their racks, Wills's read "Prince William." And true to form, he was scrutinized more than any student before or after him. His behavior, his academic progress, his friendships with other boys; all were widely reported for all the world to read about. While some coverage was complimentary, much was not. It was pointed out that in Wetherby's academic tracking system (called streaming), William did not qualify for the brightest group, but was placed in with the average kids. Strangely enough, William's father counted that a plus. Prince Charles is reported, in *People* magazine, to have said, "Being too bright can be a disadvantage for the sort of life that William has before him. I would like to try and bring up our children to be well mannered, to think of other people, to put themselves in other people's positions. That way, even if they turn out not to be very bright or well-qualified, at least if they have reasonable manners, they will get so much further in life than if they did not have any at all."

Compassion did seem to come naturally to William, and as his father said, that trait serves a leader well. A Wetherby schoolmate's mother reported, "I've often seen Prince William comforting a young child who's clearly unhappy. He'll talk earnestly to him and make sure he's all right before resuming playing. He really does think of others."

William's tenure at Wetherby, however, was also marked by some questionable behavior. As befits a future monarch, he did seem to be developing a "take charge" attitude. One observer said, "Prince William can be a really bossy-boots. He is a natural leader and likes to take command. He likes to organize games of tag that can get quite boisterous."

Alas, it was at Wetherby that he earned yet another nickname: William the Terrible and/or Billy Basher. His skill in tearing things apart had only improved over the years. And he'd developed a new one: intimidation. It was snitched that, if thwarted, he threatened the other boys. Some of what he reportedly said is no different from what millions of kids have boasted over generations, the ever-popular: "My daddy can beat up your daddy." Except William noted that his daddy was the Prince of Wales. Worse, the tiny terror allegedly added, "When I'm King I'm going to send my knights round to kill you!"

Again, such childish threats are not uncommon, nor usually taken seriously; they certainly wouldn't have made news were they not uttered by Prince William, who was beginning to realize his unique position in the world and the power he would someday wield. "William knows he's special," said a visitor to the family's Highgrove estate. "He's incredibly confident for a little boy his age."

Sometimes, Princess Diana would accompany the

detective who drove William to school. Although she rarely picked him up at the end of the day, she was often at home when he returned in the afternoons. William's home life had continued apace. He was into all things quite normal—digging up worms in the garden, adopting a pet rabbit he'd found on the property at Highgrove, playing soccer, and adding to his prodigious collection of toy guns and swords, Thundercats, and Transformers. He loved going to the zoo with his nanny, where he was often treated to ice-cream cones and lollipops.

Additionally, William was into all things quite privileged—posing for official portraits, going for trips in the queen's private aircraft with his father at the controls, and taking deluxe vacations. When he was six, he and his family rode bikes on the Isles of Scilly, off the coast of Cornwall.

Prince William's favorite activity at this stage of his life was riding his pony, Trigger. He was becoming quite a proficient rider, too. He competed in his first horse show in 1988 and won a rosette as third best young rider at his level. A few months later he snagged another for "best turned-out" young rider.

A love of horses is something he had in common with his grandmother, Queen Elizabeth. That was the main topic of conversation whenever he and Granny, as he'd learned to call her, got together. The queen, an accomplished equestrienne, often couldn't keep pace with her grandson. "William trotted along so fast on his pony," she once said, "I could barely keep up." She clearly cherished him. As an insider once observed, "William has inherited his mother's beguiling manner along with the Spencer looks, and like most of the women in his life, his grandmother simply adores him."

It was on his pony, along the trails at Highgrove, that William was often sighted in those years, waving good morning to the steady stream of guests who came to visit his parents. He'd even acknowledge the lucky sightseers, who could just barely see the estate from a public footpath that runs by the grounds. Naturally, William was quite used to the dignitaries, officers, and heads of state who came to visit his father. What he wasn't used to were the rock stars— or one in particular. Though he probably looks back on this incident and blushes today, when William was six, rocker Bob Geldof visited Prince Charles and Princess Diana. William's shocked reaction was, "Why does he have such dirty hair, Daddy? Why is he wearing gym shoes?"

Although Prince Charles still spent a prodigious amount of time on the road with official state business, when he was home, William was often by his side. The little prince loved to accompany his dad to Smiths Lawn at Windsor, where Prince Charles often played polo on the weekends. There, he'd watch his father play, and run onto the field between chukkas and give "Poppa" a hug. But the most fun for Wills was feeding the polo ponies and sometimes even sneaking a lump of sugar for himself or Harry.

Spending time with both parents was a rare commodity—it would become almost obsolete, but

Prince William was voted the most handsome royal. It's easy to see why. *(All Action/Retna, Ltd.)*

Toddler Wills climbs aboard a fire engine, 1988. *(Photographers Int'l/ Shooting Star)*

Wills (far right) strikes a pose on the ski slopes of Klosters, Switzerland, alongside his brother and father, January 1996. *(Justin Goff, Camerapress, Retna, Ltd.)*

In 1989, Wills loved to visit his father, Prince Charles, on the polo field at Smiths Lawn in Windsor. (*Photographers Int'l/Shooting Star*)

When William entered Eton College, he posed
with his family and the school's house-master,
Dr. Andrew Gailey. *(All Action/Retna, Ltd.)*

Prince William wasn't the first royal teen idol. Back in 1965, his father, then a teenager, was featured in America's *16 Magazine*. (*Courtesy* 16 Magazine)

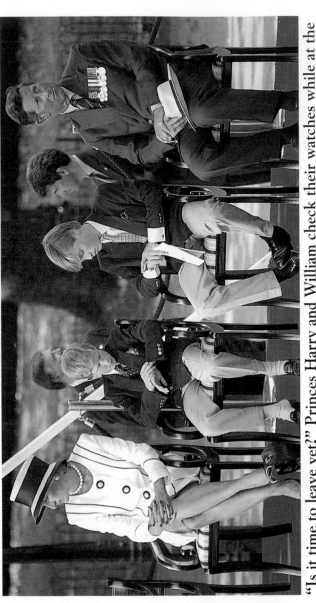

"Is it time to leave yet?" Princes Harry and William check their watches while at the official procession of war veterans on England's VJ weekend. (*All Action/Retna, Ltd.*)

When Prince William is with his father, Prince Charles, he often dresses in conservative suit and tie. *(All Action/Retna, Ltd.)*

Hanging out after classes with his buddies on Eton High Street, near his school in Windsor.
(All Action/Retna, Ltd.)

Wills and his schoolmates wear the Eton College uniform.
(Richard Gillard, Camerapress, Retna, Ltd.)

of course Wills didn't know that then—and at that time the family made the most of being together. In their apartments at Kensington, or behind the wrought-iron gates of their Highgrove retreat, they often ate breakfast and lunch *en famille*. William and Harry were encouraged to have playmates over, including their older cousins Peter and Zara, but discouraged from doing something else most kids consider normal: watching TV. "Too much television is bad," their father opined. "It robs children of their imaginativeness." In fact, Prince Charles cited storytelling ability as the chief reason he'd asked his friend Sir Laurens van der Post to be William's godfather. "He is one of the best storytellers I have ever come across, and I want my son to be able to sit on his godfather's knee and listen to his wonderful stories."

Aside from visits with his godfather (who passed away in December 1996) William also spent time with his grandparents—not only the queen and Prince Philip, but also those on his mom's side, Frances Shand Kydd and the Earl of Spencer. Diana's dad once admitted of his grandson, "William is high-spirited, energetic, and always getting into trouble. But you can't get annoyed with him, no matter how naughty he's been, because he's got such charm."

When Wills was seven, his brother Harry joined him at Wetherby. Naturally, their relationship at school was commented upon, and of course, comparisons of the boys began in earnest. "Like any pair of siblings," wrote *Redbook* magazine, "William and

Harry sometimes don't get along. Still, the two boys are close. William is protective of his little brother." Harry, though deemed the brighter of the two and immediately placed in the highest academic grouping, was reported to be in awe of Wills.

Although their parents took pains to treat the boys equally, making certain they adhered to the same rules and were given the same education, the brothers still had reason to be jealous of each other. William, after all, will someday be king, and as such will inherit the biggest portion of their father's considerable wealth. But he'll pay a price, with constant intrusions on his privacy, which Harry will not have to suffer. The "spare" will be afforded the luxury of a private life. It doesn't seem to have been prompted by jealousy, but once William did dangle hapless Harry by his feet out of a Windsor Castle window—ostensibly so his brother could get a better view.

Misguided or not, William was beginning to take responsibility for his brother and, in doing so, demonstrated his own growing maturity. At his next public affair, the wedding of his mother's cousin, he was chosen as a page boy. Instead of disrupting the proceedings as he'd done in the past, he helped organize Harry and the other small pages and bridesmaids. "Get back! Get in line!" Wills urged them. Indeed, with Harry, William sometimes acted like a third parent. Once William caught him sticking his tongue out to reporters after a visit to see their newborn cousin Beatrice (Sarah and Prince

Andrew's daughter). William grabbed Harry and hissed, "Stop it, Harry! That's very naughty."

Yet, just a little while later, at an amusement park, William instructed his brother on the best, fastest way to get down a slide. "He looked after Harry and was gentle with him," reported an onlooker.

Clearly, Prince William was maturing and, as he approached his mid-childhood years, was coming to understand all too well that he wasn't just another kid.

Prince Charles once said, "People expect a great deal of us, but the moment someone puts you on a pedestal, along comes a separate brigade that likes knocking you off." Whether those exact words of wisdom about the vagaries of fame were ever whispered to William isn't known. Most probably, he figured it out on his own. If he hadn't prior to his eighth birthday, this incident no doubt brought it home. William's privacy was so invaded that a reporter caught him with his pants down—literally—peeing in a bush in a wooded area near his school. The humiliation of being spied upon is one thing; it's quite another when it runs as a two-page spread in a newspaper under the heading THE ROYAL WEE.

As much as any other, that experience led William to much more circumspect public behavior. Where he was once outgoing and loved the spotlight, William became wary and mistrusting. Ironically, his change of attitude actually garnered him a more positive image. "He's begun to shed his willfulness and trade mischief for manners," was the new conventional Wills wisdom.

One magazine pinpointed this time in William's life when the truth really began to dawn on him. "He's now going through a phase few people experience, a period of recognizing that he has been set apart by destiny."

William's most immediate destiny involved his education. At the age of eight, he was ready to graduate from the Wetherby School and go on. Originally, Princess Diana had been opposed to sending him away to boarding school, because she and Charles both had miserable experiences at their respective away-from-home schools. Besides, Diana just liked having William home. "The best part of my day is getting home to the children," she once said. But when it came time for William to advance to the next level of his education, it became apparent, even to Diana, that boarding school was probably the best move. For one thing, security concerns made continuing in day school too difficult. For another, they knew that the earlier William learned to become independent, the better. To Americans, the idea of being sent away to school at eight years old may sound cruel, but most people who've been through the English private school system agree that if you don't start early, adjusting to boarding school later on is that much harder. It's like learning to ride a two-wheeler; the younger you start, the easier it is to get the hang of it.

And by that time in his life, there's a good chance William was ready to fly the coop anyway. For as much as he, Harry, and their parents continued to symbolize a unified, joyous family in public, William was probably beginning to suspect another truth. His parents, in fact, were not getting along, and the fights between them were more frequent and threatening to become public. He was only eight, but it's a good bet he realized even then that getting away wasn't such a bad idea.

Chapter Five

Leading Two Lives

A boarding school may have been decided on, but the right one for Prince William was the subject of much debate, in the press and behind palace doors. Great Britain has many high-caliber academies, including Gordonstoun in Scotland, where Prince Charles had gone. And after an intense search, it was announced that William would attend an exclusive preparatory school called Ludgrove. While it was a full-time boarding school, he would only board there on weekdays. Once Friday came around, the young prince could head home for the weekends, since Ludgrove was in Berkshire, only twenty-five miles from London. That arrangement made his mother very happy.

But geography wasn't the only plus Ludgrove had

going for it. It very much came with its own pedigree. The hundred-year-old establishment has educated many royals and aristocrats, including the Duke of Kent and Sarah Ferguson's (William's aunt) father, Major Ronald Ferguson. Perhaps even more important, the all-boys' Ludgrove is considered a "feeding station" to Eton, one of the most famous and prestigious prep schools in Britain. Sending William to Ludgrove, which reportedly cost four thousand dollars per term, was a sign that his parents had perhaps already decided on the future course of his education.

It's doubtful William was thinking about any of that, however, September 10, 1990, his first day of boarding school. The retinue of photojournalists outside the school to greet him had by now become familiar. This time wary William neither waved nor struck a coy pose for the cameras, however, but entered the school much like other students. William arrived with both parents and, sandwiched between them, shook hands with the school's headmaster, then headed for his dorm room. Much was made of the fact that although the threesome seemingly arrived together, Charles had actually arrived in one car, while Diana and William came in another and switched into Charles's car just before turning into the school's driveway. After depositing William, in what was called a "well-staged appearance," they left separately and did not see each other again for thirty-nine days.

As it was at his other schools, some of William's

experiences at Ludgrove would be very typical; others, completely out of the ordinary. "We shall treat Prince William exactly the same way as the other pupils," remarked the headmaster on the day of the future king's arrival, and every attempt was made to do just that.

Wills was called a "squit," which is the older boys' nickname for the new boys. He had to wear Ludgrove's official navy blue uniform every day. He also was subject to all the same rules and regulations and had to use the same facilities as the other 186 students enrolled there. That included sharing a dorm room with four other boys, getting up at 7:15 A.M., using the communal bathroom, eating breakfast in the dining room, attending classes, and adhering to the "lights out by 8 P.M." rule. Phone calls home were prohibited. Along with his peers, William took classes in the basics—reading, writing, arithmetic, plus electives like art, French, and carpentry. Sports facilities on the 130-acre campus included a swimming pool, tennis courts, and a nine-hole golf course.

What William didn't share with his peers was the manner in which he was addressed. While Ludgrove typically calls students by their surnames, the young prince was simply called William. And it's safe to say that no other students came with a group of bodyguards, whose job it was to watch over him day and night. That situation caused one local resident of the town to grouse that it seemed "an awful lot of fuss for one small boy."

The small boy had done a lot of maturing by the

time he got to Ludgrove. Caught-on-camera incidents of bad behavior—including trying to pinch a teacher's butt—were few and far between. Instead of terrorizing schoolmates with retaliatory tales of what he'd do when he was king, William was popular from the start. He participated in all school activities, including soccer tournaments, where Diana was often photographed cheering him on in the stands, and once, comforting him on the field after a loss. Like most other mothers, she turned up on the special days parents were encouraged to visit. Diana took second place in a Mother's Race at Ludgrove and doubled with William in a mother-son tennis tournament. Perhaps as a thank-you, William phoned his mom's favorite restaurant and made a reservation for her as a surprise. He was only nine at the time.

Still, the constant glare of the spotlight was beginning to affect him. According to an insider, "William has an image of himself and therefore is worried about making a fool of himself."

If William was settling into an enjoyable routine at school, he was finding life at home anything but routine. For the home Wills got to go to at the end of each week had become one divided. His parents, who hadn't yet officially separated, *had* begun to lead separate lives, and by 1991, William began what would be years of bouncing between them. When not on the road, Charles could usually be found at his private quarters in London's St. James Palace, or at Balmoral in Scotland. Diana was most often at Kensington Palace in London. Both occupied their country residence at Highgrove, but hardly ever at the same time.

Admittedly, William spent a lot less time with his father, who was publicly criticized for being the less attentive and therefore "worse" parent. According to one widely circulated anecdote, on his very first week-long break from Ludgrove, "William raced happily into his father's palace study in London, only to find it empty. William burst into tears, until Diana promptly called Charles, who was in Balmoral, and asked him to fax his son a 'welcome home' message." After that, faxing became a frequent method of father-son communication. A worker at Highgrove described William "delightedly standing by the machine, watching his father's messages as they slowly appeared."

Charles's distance from both his sons was becoming an issue, but it didn't mean William spent no time with his dad. Indeed, one of Charles's friends said that it was a case of quality over quantity time: "When [Charles] does see the boys, he's all over them. But then, he might not choose to see them again for a month or so." Another added, "Charles is treating William pretty much the same way his own father, Philip, treated Charles"—in other words, they just didn't see very much of each other.

No matter how rare, William's visits with his dad were well chronicled. They usually involved the kinds of outdoorsy activities for which the royal family is known to be passionate: hunting, fishing, shooting, and riding. All of which Wills seemed to enjoy and even excel at. With his father, he dressed in the conservative style expected of a future monarch and took his meals, which were prepared by the palace staff, at home. Aside from traditional fare like sausages and fruitcake, William was encouraged to eat organically grown produce from Charles's farms. His dad was becoming quite a dedicated environmentalist, and Wills was indoctrinated early on.

The people around his father were different than those Diana hung out with, and William soon became well acquainted with them. They included Tiggy Legge-Bourke, whom Charles had hired as the nanny when the kids were with him, and Camilla Parker-Bowles, an old friend of his father's who would eventually play a much larger and more public role in his life. It couldn't have been easy for William to know that as much as his father liked and trusted these women, Diana couldn't abide either of them. If William liked them, which he reportedly did, he might have felt disloyal to his mother. A conflict had thus begun that would haunt him for years to come.

Life with Mom, who appeared to be the more attentive—by far—parent, was entirely different. Doting Diana, it is said, arranged her schedule around William's and Harry's. "She has never failed to collect William personally from school for his weekends off," reported royal watchers. It was with Mom that Wills and Harry got to do the fun things most kids take for granted. They went to amusement parks, they went skiing; they hit the fast-food restaurants and went to the movies. William went to a custom car show and got to sit behind the wheel of a $100,000 Ferrari convertible. With Diana, Wills could wear jeans, sweatshirts, high-tops, and a baseball cap, much like his mom did on their informal outings.

Because William loved riding so much, Diana reportedly tried to overcome her own fear—which dated back to when she was five and thrown off a horse—to take lessons. William attended horse shows and progressed to more advanced riding lessons with a new instructor. Major James Hewitt, a Gulf War hero and equestrian stationed at Buckingham Palace, was hired by Diana for that purpose. William befriended his new coach; unfortunately, Major Hewitt later betrayed many family confidences. There was a similar situation when Diana took William to see rugby star Will Carling play: A man they both befriended eventually turned into yet another untrustworthy enemy.

In spite of the split between Charles and Diana, one thing did unite the fractured family: William's training as a future monarch. The year William started Ludgrove was the year he took his first formal steps into the world of like-it-or-not royal duties and public appearances. These were officially sanctioned "put your best foot forward" photo ops. In 1990 he accompanied his mom during a Kensington Palace reception and shook hands with 180 dignitaries. He got dressed up and attended musicals with his mother; he joined his family for official portraits to be distributed around the world. In preparation for his future role, which will involve a lot of speechmaking, Wills learned to give the customary "thank you and farewell" speech to any departing household staff member.

March 1, 1991, marked William's first real official engagement. He was granted the day off from Ludgrove to travel to the city of Cardiff, in Wales. Prince William's "job" was to unveil a six-foot-high plaque promoting the commerce and culture of Cardiff—and yes, it probably was as boring as it sounds. But Wills carried out his duties like a trooper. He wore a yellow daffodil, in honor of St. David's Day, the national day of Wales, shook innumerable hands, and "worked the crowd" of over 2,500. He blushed when one little girl handed him a bouquet of flowers, and again when a sixty-six-year-old woman leaned over the barricade and kissed him on the cheek. At one point Diana asked him how he was holding up; Wills reportedly replied, "How much longer is this going to last?"

Another step in William's royal apprenticeship was his growing awareness of charitable causes, something Diana had become quite famous for. She felt it important that Wills and Harry understand that the world around them was filled with people less fortunate than themselves. Diana candidly put it this way: "I want [William and Harry] to experience what most people already know—that they are growing up in a multiracial society in which everyone is not rich, or has four holidays a year, or speaks standard English and drives a Range Rover."

Diana was most dedicated to those charities involving children, especially seriously disabled kids, those with AIDS, or those fighting drug addictions. In the early nineties Diana held the titles of president, patron, or commander-in-chief of ninety-one different organizations. She also held the unofficial title of "hardest-working royal." Princess Diana's involvement in any charity brings with it a ton of publicity—and with that, a lot more money is generally showered on the charity. Diana's enduring popularity no doubt stems from both her selflessness and her tangible contributions.

Family strife and official duties notwithstanding, William still got to have a lot of fun and enjoy plenty of princely perks. There were those several vacations each year, including a memorable one in the Virgin Islands with his cousins Peter and Zara. Peter, who was four years older than Wills, was teaching his young cousin the sport of cricket.

If Prince William expressed interest in something, he usually got to experience it. His fascination with guns and all things military goes back to his toddler days. When he was ten, he was given his own child-sized replica of a uniform worn in the Parachute Regiment, of which his father is colonel in chief. Wills was also made an "official" member of the regiment for a day. Suited up in camouflage gear, he learned to handle a gun and ate soldier's food, which he professed to like very much.

But many of Wills's young pleasures were quite simple and ordinary. He loved to ride his BMX bike around the grounds of his various homes; he skateboarded with his friends and even did "touristy" things like visiting the Tower of London and the spooky London Dungeon, a grisly waxworks exhibit. William also enjoyed children's theater performances and once volunteered during an audience-participation play where he was chosen to help blow up balloons. Aside from riding lessons, he took private instruction in tennis, swimming, rugby, and piano.

A favorite sport continued to be "let's elude the bodyguards." William took great pleasure in confounding his security detail by hiding behind bushes or mounting his pony at Balmoral and riding off by himself. After trying to ditch his bodyguards once too often, he was given an electronic homing device to wear—so his location could be pinpointed at any time. Pinpointing his location was of little help, however, the day William and Harry, playing at their uncle Andrew's estate, locked themselves in a "terrorist-proof dungeon." The boys couldn't get out and screamed for help. Andrew had to call Scotland Yard, which sent a messenger with a special key to free the boys.

In spite of that bit of mischief, and the fact that he'd wrecked the expensive toy Jaguar he'd been given as a younger child, William's positive reputation was continuing to evolve. Few people were referring to him as willful and wild; the adjectives more likely to be used were *self-confident* and *independent*. Those traits would come in handy, as his parents' personal life continued to come apart, every day more publicly.

Chapter Six

He Said, She Said

*I*n an age of trash TV and tabloids run amuck, it's not unusual for the private lives of world leaders to be trumpeted all over the headlines. However, that wasn't the way it always was—in either the USA or Britain. For better or worse, there used to be a time when the private lives of our presidents, elected officials, monarchs, and other dignitaries was not grist for the gossip mill. Such was the case throughout the first decade of Prince Charles and Princess Diana's marriage. While many of their secrets, including their marital strife, were known by insiders, little was leaked to the press. The public was aware, of course, that the royal couple were leading increasingly separate lives, but nothing really damaging to their reputations had been reported.

All that changed in mid-1991. Suddenly it was as if the protective "kid gloves" came off and anything went as far as reporting on the royals, complimentary, or more often, not. What happened to cause the switch? Most royals-watchers point to an incident involving Prince William, who, through no fault of his own, became the unwitting catalyst for the change in the media's attitude toward his parents.

The incident was William's head injury, an accident that happened at Ludgrove on Monday, June 3, 1991. Wills and some friends were fooling around on the school's golf course. One of the boys was absentmindedly swinging a golf club around like a baseball bat—William's head accidentally got in the way. William, just shy of his ninth birthday, was knocked to the ground. Blood was seeping from a gash on his forehead. Naturally, his bodyguards weren't far, and they rushed him by police car to the nearby Royal Berkshire Hospital.

William's parents were notified immediately and, by all accounts, both sped to the hospital; Princess Diana from Kensington, Prince Charles from Highgrove. They got there just as Wills was being wheeled in for a CAT scan (an internal X-ray of his head) and both stayed by his side, reassuring him that he'd be okay. The results of the X-ray showed that Wills had suffered a depressed fracture of the skull (a slight indentation of the bone) on the left forehead and needed to be operated on.

In spite of the call for surgery, Prince William was

never in any grave danger, nor was he ever unconscious. Indeed, while being transferred to Great Ormond Street Hospital in London for the operation, he was reportedly "brave, chatty, and chirpy" during the ambulance ride, on which Diana accompanied him. Charles followed in his car.

The operation, performed to push out the dent in his head and check for bone splinters and lacerations, took seventy minutes and was declared a complete success. William stayed in the hospital for two nights following the surgery. His mom was by his side the entire time and on the third day took him home. Charles, however, did not display such dedication to his firstborn. It was reported that before William's operation even began, Charles left the hospital to go to the opera. There, he told his companions that William's condition was "not too bad." After the performance Prince Charles departed for an environmental conference being held the next day in the northern part of the country. While Charles kept in touch with Wills by phone, and visited his son the next evening, he was vilified in the media for his lack of concern.

Previously, many reporters had hinted that Charles was an absentee dad, but none had really come down hard on the Prince of Wales, usually citing the royal duties and tradition that took precedence over parenting. However, Charles's nonchalance at William's accident changed all that: There was little even the most sympathetic reports could do to repair Charles's image as an absent or, worse, uncaring parent. WHAT KIND OF DAD ARE YOU?

reprimanded the headlines of one paper. The story went on to accuse, "What sort of father of an eight-year-old boy, nearly brained by a golf club, leaves the hospital before knowing the outcome, for a night at the opera?"

After that incident a torrent of anti-Charles articles followed. William's dad was bashed in story after story accusing him of being more interested in the environment, architecture, and polo than in spending time with his children. One columnist said, "Charles is beginning to treat his sons like well-fed pets who know their place in the world of their utterly self-involved parent. Certainly, it must hurt William and Harry to see their father more often on TV than in the flesh."

It's more likely that what stung William more were the public put-downs of his family. For by the age of nine he could no longer be completely shielded from what was being written and whispered about his parents. Although no TV or newspapers were allowed at Ludgrove, gossip always has a way of leaking in. Worse, perhaps, Charles and Diana themselves appeared to be active participants in the mudslinging. Not that either parent gave personal interviews, but by sanctioning various "close friends" and/or "palace insiders" to make their point of view public, they very much used the media as a battleground to blast each other and try to sway public opinion.

Each "side" had its cadre of partisans, who gladly planted stories in the press trying to make one or the other parent look good/bad. And every time one side made a claim, the other counterclaimed it. It was all like a bizarre "nah-nah-nah-nah-nah" game of one-up-manship. It was all nasty and distasteful; none of it could really be hidden from William or Harry, who had to withstand volley after volley of mortifying revelations about their parents—pretty much supplied *by* their parents. While some children of divorce can probably relate to the ill will between parents, it's hard to imagine it all splashed across headlines the world over. Which is exactly the situation Wills had to endure. In fact, he still does.

The anti-Charles faction claimed that not only was he an irresponsible and uncaring father, the Prince of Wales was also an uncaring and irresponsible husband who preferred the company of other women—specifically his old friend Camilla Parker-Bowles—to his wife. The anti-Di forces responded with the equivalent of "if his wife shared some of his interests, and tried harder to make the marriage happy, the prince wouldn't spend so much time away."

Charles's pals then attacked Diana for not being more sympathetic when her husband suffered a severely broken arm after a polo accident; Di's buds responded that Charles's own sympathy was in short supply when dealing with his wife's far more debilitating eating disorder.

Di's minions accused Charles of becoming self-absorbed, gloomy, and indifferent to public opinion; Charles's partisans counterattacked that Diana was "sullen, brainless, and empty-headed." She said he and his friends were "crashing bores"; he said she and her friends were extravagant shoppers and obsessive partygoers.

Hard to believe that it went on, but it did—for years. Charles was chastised for not acknowledging Diana's thirtieth birthday, which coincided with their tenth wedding anniversary; he countered that he wanted to make a party, but she refused. His side also insisted that Diana "thwarts his attempts to see the children and increasingly keeps them away from him." To which Diana's friends answered that when he *was* in their company, Charles was reluctant to touch or hug his sons.

For the most part, Diana was still being portrayed as the sainted single mother of the future king; the one who, according to public opinion, "proved herself the steadier parent and better half of the future monarchy." Charles's side replied that he was tired of the public perception that Diana was the saint and he the sinner; she was just the better manipulator of the media, while their man chose to remain decorous.

Queen Elizabeth herself attempted to repair the damage by summoning the warring parties to Buckingham Palace for a pep talk. Reportedly, the gist of what she said was, "It's okay to live apart, but it must be done with discretion, never forgetting one's duty to the throne." Spin control by the Palace was then attempted, but backfired when the prince and princess undertook two tours together. In both Canada and South Korea, they gave each other the public cold shoulder. The disastrous joint visits were chronicled throughout the world.

Although Prince William has so far not said anything publicly about how all the mudslinging made him feel, one anecdote is rather telling. Reacting to a particularly brutal anti-Di article he'd found, William reportedly "burst into tears and wailed, 'How can they do this to mummy? Why can't daddy protect her?'"

It isn't hard to empathize with William about the entire situation—his mother says one thing and slams his father; his father contradicts it and disses his mother. Both are publicly humiliated. Yet William loved them both. No amount of money, princely perks, or promises of future power could insulate William from hurt and humiliation.

The public squabbling continued and gave way, inevitably, to speculation about the future of Prince Charles and Princess Diana's marriage. In 1992 a Palace source was quoted as saying, "I believe the marriage is stone dead. I don't think there is animosity between them, it's worse . . . they just don't care." The "will they or won't they/should they or shouldn't they" separate official debate had begun and, once started, raged on loudly.

Naturally, if Charles and Diana were almost any other couple, if their marriage did not involve the succession to the British throne, there's little doubt they would have divorced long ago. But a split such as theirs guaranteed major ramifications, involving the future of a centuries old and deeply revered tradition, the British monarchy.

Nevertheless, separate they did, formally—many said, finally!—in December 1992. The timing of the announcement, just before William and Harry's Christmas break from school, was deliberate. It was hoped the worst of the media coverage would be over before the young princes got out of school, where they were less likely to be exposed to the brunt of it. Just prior to the public announcement, Diana went to Ludgrove herself to break the news to her sons. The boys were ushered into the headmaster's office so they and their mom could have some privacy as she explained what was about to happen—the announcement and then the new arrangements in their lives. According to one report, Prince William burst out crying at the news. According to another, he dried his tears and stoically said, "I hope you'll both be happier now."

The official announcement was made by British Prime Minister John Major in the House of Commons (the branch of government similar to the U.S. House of Representatives). In a carefully worded release, it asserted that the decision by Prince Charles and Princess Diana to separate had been reached amicably; that the family would continue to appear in public together from time to time for family occasions and national events. It also assured the British public that "the succession to the throne was unaffected . . . (aside from Charles's ascension) there is no reason why the Princess of Wales should not be crowned queen in due course."

The effect of that part of the announcement was not what the Palace expected. Instead of placating the public, it prompted an outcry that despite Diana's personal popularity, the British people overwhelmingly no longer wanted her to be queen: 80 percent of five hundred people polled rejected the idea of Queen Di. In fact, after the announcement, several instant TV polls were taken. Even though they were against the separated Diana being able to ascend, still twice as many people blamed Charles for the collapse of the marriage. While 57 percent sympathized with Diana, only 12 percent had any empathy for the Prince of Wales.

Questions regarding Prince Charles's own ascension to the throne quickly followed. For one thing, an official separation already undermined Charles's position as heir to the throne. For another, should a divorce ensue, it was said back then, his possibilities looked even worse. As king, he would automatically be head of the Church of England, a church that frowns upon divorce.

Many felt that no matter what happened, after all the years of negative press, Charles was not fit to be king anyway. But if not Charles, then who? All eyes turned to William—and he was only ten! In fact, as early as 1992, there was talk of Wills ascending instead of his father. Political leader John Bowis opined, "If it is not possible to have a happy monarch and family, I think we should skip a generation and wait for William." Some went further and said that Prince Charles might consider willingly removing himself from the line of succession.

Talk about pressure! Clearly, his parents' formal separation put a huge amount on William. Not only was he now being looked to as his country's future sovereign, in some circles he was even being touted as the savior of the entire steeped-in-history tradition. "It will be the character and skills of Prince William that determine the fate of the monarchy in the twenty-first century," proclaimed a respected royals expert.

Queen Elizabeth pronounced 1992 one of her worst years ever, and it was hardly a great one for her grandson Prince William. For aside from the family strife, that was the year the future king also became a pawn—he was his mother's best and only weapon in her battle with the Windsors, who of course took Charles's side on everything. But as long as Diana remained close with her son (and why wouldn't she?), the ruling family could not be too harsh with her. On top of all that upheaval in his life, William also suffered the private pain of the death of his grandfather, Diana's dad, the Earl of Spencer, in March of that year.

William hoped the new year would be a brighter one, and in certain ways it was—some parts of his life actually returned to "normal." Indeed, to all outward appearances, it seemed that Wills and Harry had adapted to the official split. Both, now at Ludgrove, seemed to enjoy school. Academically, William's performance improved, and he spent most of his time there in the top third of his class.

As per the separation agreement, William and Harry were now legally required to spend equal amounts of time with both parents. Equal—but very different, of course. As they had been prior to the separation, William and Harry's days with Diana usually involved some kind of fun. She took them to the huge video game arcade at London's Piccadilly Circus (which isn't a circus as Americans know it, but one of the busiest districts in London, like New York City's Times Square); she took them go-carting, on water slides, and to her favorite restaurant, San Lorenzo. Wills attended Britain's most famous pro tennis match at Wimbledon, where afterward, winner Steffi Graf offered to give him lessons. Vacations with mom included beach trips to the Caribbean (where, it was noted, they flew by commercial airline), skiing vacations in Austria, and a sightseeing trip to Ontario's Niagara Falls.

Ironically, William ended up spending more time with his father after the separation than he had before; scheduled visits now were compulsory. Not that either Wills or Harry seemed to mind spending time with Prince Charles. In spite of everything that has been said about the fractured family, there is no evidence William ever stopped loving and respecting his father. Visits with Prince Charles were most often taken at Highgrove or Balmoral. There, both boys rode their ponies around the country estates and practiced their shooting and fishing skills. One such fly-fishing outing with dad was covered for a television documentary honoring Charles's twenty-fifth year as Prince of Wales.

There were even occasions when William's parents spent time together—albeit on his behalf. When William appeared in the school play, as historical warrior Napoleon Bonaparte, both were in the audience; it marked their first public appearance together since the official split. As soon as the play ended, Charles left for Highgrove, where he continued to reside on the weekends; Diana took the boys back to her primary residence, Kensington Palace.

Charles and Diana joined forces for William's eleventh birthday party, where the theme was America's West. All the guests dressed as cowboys, including William's parents. Afterward, they both agreed to allow him to spend a few summer weeks with a friend at a Montana ranch in the USA, far away from the prying eyes of the British media. There, William learned to ride cowboy style, to lasso, and even to square-dance. He made a good impression on his U.S. hosts, who declared Prince William's horsemanship impressive, his manners and friendliness even more so.

Naturally, however, William had become even more wary of people's motives in getting friendly with him. By the age of eleven he'd asked his friends to hide any notes or letters he'd written them. "William is old beyond his years," said the parent of one of his schoolmates.

Other things had changed drastically since his parents' formal separation. For the first time ever, in 1993, Prince William did not attend Easter services at Buckingham Palace with his grandmother, the queen. Instead, Diana took the boys to the European Grand Prix auto races that day. For the first time the family's Christmas card (in 1992) did not feature a portrait of the foursome, but simply William—sitting, it was noted, on a throne-like chair—with

Harry beside him. And for the first time William did not spend Christmas day with his mother, who opted to be with her family, the Althorp-Spencers, while Wills and Harry took part in the traditional royal family gathering at the queen's 20,500-acre Sandringham estate.

William continued to take on more royal duties, including such state functions as the fiftieth anniversary of V-J day. William won accolades for his professional handling of the situation. "He's very self-possessed" was the verdict of his performance. Diana still had many official engagements on her calendar, and after the separation William took his father's place by Diana's side for many of them. At her Christmas party for the staff at Kensington Palace, it was Wills who got up and made the traditional thank-you speech.

He'd also become quite savvy when it came to the press. On a skiing holiday with his mom and brother, William refused to pose for photographers who'd upset Diana the day before.

And interestingly enough, William even managed to be the center of his very own controversy. In May 1993 he went on a hunting expedition, which wasn't unusual for him, but this time roused the ire of animal rights groups, who blasted, "If his father wants him to go out and shoot animals, he should buy him a good camera." It should be noted that hunting and shooting are considered very normal and not immoral activities to certain people, including most of England's upper-class country squire gentlemen. Like their father and hundreds of ancestors before him, Wills and Harry have been brought up this way. The shooting controversy, however, would continue to dog him for many years to come. William was far from unaware of it—or its consequences for those he cared about. Back in 1994 Princess Diana was offered the presidency of an organization called the Royal Society for the Prevention of Cruelty to Animals. "You can't take it," young William advised her. "Every time I kill something, they'll blame you."

Chapter Seven

On to Eton

The years immediately following Prince Charles and Princess Diana's official separation were relatively peaceful—for Wills, anyway. While the "War of the Windsors," as it was tagged, raged on, he and Harry settled into a familiar pattern. Both adapted well to life at Ludgrove and to their split lives bouncing between their parents. With few exceptions, they continued to observe most holidays in the traditional way.

The royal family has always celebrated Christmas at Sandringham, and with or without Diana present—since the separation, she has spent some years there, and some not—Wills and Harry continued to do just that. The sacred family holiday is always celebrated the exact same way every year:

with a black-tie dinner, church service, and pheasant shoot. Those present include Wills's grandparents Queen Elizabeth and Prince Philip; his great grandmother, the Queen Mum, a host of aunts, uncles, cousins—including Peter and Zara Phillips and the little Princesses Beatrice and Eugenie (daughters of the now-divorced Prince Andrew and Sarah Ferguson)—and, of course, his father, Prince Charles, plus assorted guests.

There is a huge Christmas tree, with presents piled under it, which, according to this family's tradition, are opened Christmas Eve instead of the following morning. The gifts, however, aren't as extravagant as the family is used to receiving from well-wishers: instead, the Windsor tradition is to exchange gifts that are "cheap and cheerful, and best of all funny." In previous years that has included a musical toilet-paper holder and a leopard-skin shower cap.

The family's humongous Christmas Eve dinner is a formal affair. Everyone must dress to the nines. However, Wills, Harry, and their younger cousins don't attend it. They have their own kids' dinner—called a "nursery tea"—in another wing of the mansion.

Windsors of all ages join together Christmas day to attend services at St. Mary Magdalene Church. It's a very public event, as the family members often walk to church and are hailed by thousands of their subjects every step of the way. After services and lunch the family gathers round the television to watch Queen Elizabeth's annual Christmas broadcast, during which she addresses the nation—one of the myriad royal duties William will someday inherit.

A more pressing matter, of course, once again concerned Wills's further schooling. In spite of Charles and Diana's horrendously public squabbling, the decision of where their son would take the next step up the educational ladder was one they made together. The decision wasn't a difficult one. By enrolling him in Ludgrove, they'd pretty well decided years earlier that he'd eventually matriculate to Eton.

Eton College, as it's called, is the American equivalent of a high school. Located right near Windsor Castle, it is one of England's most exclusive and expensive "public"—meaning private—schools, and one of the country's oldest, established in 1440. Eton boasts many graduates, both famous and familial. Diana's father and brother graduated from there, as did Camilla Parker-Bowles's son, Tom. So did *1984* author George Orwell, poet Percy Bysshe Shelley, *James Bond* author Ian Fleming, plus an astounding twenty others who went on to become prime minister (a position akin to America's president).

Still, the school had never before educated a future king. And, in spite of his personal pedigree, Eton wasn't a sure bet for Wills, either. Like every other candidate for admission, he had to take a rigorous entrance exam. In a turnaround from his less than auspicious academic beginnings—when he was placed in average tracks—William finished in the top half of his class of fifteen boys in all twelve phases of Eton's difficult exam. In June 1995 his parents announced proudly that Wills would enter the school the following September and remain there for the next five years. While some have snickered that William would have gotten in anyway, others protest that the school really is academically challenging and "If he were not up to it, they would not have sent him."

Academics aside, there was every reason to believe Wills would blend in smoothly at the all-boys' Eton—and, of course, the usual glaring differences would make him stand out. On the fitting-in side, he wouldn't be the only wealthy lad at the school, by far. His classmates, some of whom matriculated from Ludgrove with him, were guaranteed to be as well-heeled, and some, as well-connected, as he; many even more so. Among the students are the children of foreign leaders and scions of Greek shipping magnates. "The students here aren't frightened of important people, nor do they resent wealthy and snobby kids," asserts a graduate. "That's who they are themselves." Gushed a longtime royals reporter, "William has that Etonian look already. The boys are burnished; they are like angels, you know, and they float around the world."

Others agree that Eton is the best possible place for William to be at this stage of his life. As one expert on England's private schools put it, "Eton is extraordinarily well suited for a boy like him—a boy who has a public future. He must make his name within the school. He can't flex his money. There is no personal expression through clothes, and cars are not allowed. Wealth or status outside the school mean little. He isn't even the only one at the school with a bodyguard! William is as near to normal at Eton as someone in his position can be."

Within the school, of course, there are various cliques. Among the senior class there are the Pops, an elite self-elected group of academic and sports leaders. Serious brainiacs call themselves the Tugs.

Like the other 240 newcomers, Wills was assigned to the school block inhabited by freshmen, called Manor House. There, his room wasn't very different from the others. Situated above the kitchen, it was small, only ten feet by seven feet, and sparse: No posters are allowed on the walls. It featured a single twin bed, nightstand, and one window. Unlike most other rooms assigned to freshmen, however, Prince William had a private bathroom—which is a pretty cool perk—and an unmarked door. Most other students have nameplates on theirs. For the record, however, William is registered at Eton as William of Wales, H.R.H. (His Royal Highness), Prince. Outside his door, one of his ever-present bodyguards is posted.

Prince William must follow the same rules as all the other boys—and there are rules for everything. If a boy is late for a class, he has to get up early the next morning and sign a tardy book. Wills wears the same uniform as the other boys—black fishtail suit and white button-down shirt with a black vest that has been the Eton staple for a hundred years—plus an extra accessory: his electronic tracking device. Barring any serious departures from form, however, Wills's bodyguards shouldn't have to track him electronically to know where he is. Like the other Etonians, he follows a highly regimented daily schedule. The young prince wakes up at 7 A.M., has breakfast among his peers an hour later, then attends chapel at 8:30. Classes start at 9 A.M. and go to 11:20 (precisely!) for a "biscuit break." They resume until 1:25 for lunch—which always consists of a meat, two vegetables, and traditional pudding.

After lunch, sports rule. Participation is compulsory, for sports are considered critical to the educational process. There are many to play at Eton, and the boys get a different-colored jersey for each. In the summer term Etonians are dubbed either "wet bobs"—which means they row on the nearby Thames River—or "dry bobs," meaning they play cricket. Then there's a sport unique to Eton, called the Wall Game, where scoring is virtually impossible because the players must huddle together against the wall. "The last goal in the Wall Game," reports *Time* magazine, "was recorded in 1909." Although he's not part of any official school team, Prince William plays soccer, water polo, and skulls (rows). After the long sports break academic classes resume at 4 P.M. until dinner.

At Eton, William studies English, chemistry, physics, biology, history, and math, plus a whopping three foreign languages: French, Greek, and Latin. If he wanted to, he could also take such diverse electives as cooking or Swahili. While Wills has made decent grades, by all accounts, he's neither nerd nor slacker but academically fits in right down the middle.

"To be cool at Eton," says a former graduate, "grades aren't important, nor is social status. What matters is an interesting personality, or being good at a sport." Wills, who excels at soccer, is definitely considered cool.

Of course, he's also definitely considered different. Aside from the ever-present bodyguard, the double-decker tour buses that slow down as they pass the school, and the local shops that sell T-shirts reading WHERE THERE'S A WILL, William stands out in other ways.

On his behalf, all newspapers and magazines at the school are vetted for hurtful stories about his parents—the offensive articles are judiciously cut out.

Perhaps more important, students and staff were warned that anyone who blabs to the press about William—no matter what the anecdote, good, bad, or indifferent—gets kicked out of the school. Even Wills's clothes are kept under lock and key, in case some prankster gets the bright idea to pilfer any item for fun or profit.

William's family put an all-points-bulletin out to the nosy newspapers, asking them not to report on him. The head of the Press Complaints commission agreed to comply and issued a statement to reporters: "The prince must be allowed to enjoy his school days, free from the fear of prying cameras. Prince William is not an institution, nor a soap star, nor a football hero. He is a child, and must be allowed to make mistakes and learn the way we all did—without reading consistently of his successes and failures in the columns of newspapers. He must be allowed to grow up away from a constant and intrusive glare."

With that, the nation's journalists were in effect barred from interviewing or photographing Wills at school—and from asking other children about him without permission from school authorities or the other students' parents.

Which didn't make the media very happy—or particularly agreeable. One newspaper editor explained, "Our readers share the country's fascination in the development of a young man who will one day be our king. I am sure that we and other newspapers will be able to record aspects of that development in a responsible manner."

Yet another journalist echoed, "William is hardly the average child and cannot expect newspapers not to be interested in his teenage years." Another suggested that tabloids were offering William's schoolmates substantial sums of money to "act as correspondents" at Eton: In other words, tell on Wills, risk expulsion, but make money.

So far, only a handful of the boys at Eton have ratted out their most famous peer. Reports have leaked that William is teased and taunted mercilessly, almost always on account of some parental indiscretion or other.

But if he's accomplished nothing else in his fifteen years, William has learned to become thick-skinned and to stand up for himself. "He's tough minded," says an insider, "and gives as good as he gets." During a rather intense snowball fight on campus, William got pelted but returned fire in kind. He has many friends, and can always count on at least one relative: his distant cousin Nicholas Knatchbull, sixteen, has become William's protector and watches out for him at Eton.

Other allies, of the friends and family variety, have visited Wills at school, including Tiggy Legge-Bourke. The woman who was originally hired by Charles to mind the boys when they were younger has become over the years more of a friend and confidante to William. Some say he can talk to her about anything, and she is always sympathetic.

Both Charles and Diana showed up at school to attend Founder's Day ceremonies, which celebrates King George III's birthday. They arrived separately and spent the morning discussing William's progress with his teachers. But to limit the opportunity for newspapers to photograph them together, William's parents refrained from taking part in the traditional event of watching the Procession of Boats.

Then there was the time, in November 1995, when Diana arrived alone. That visit was more than just a friendly "how are you" checkup. It was a very private and pointed mother-son conversation. Diana took Wills behind a tall hedge near the chapel at Eton, away from the prying eyes of any photographers, and out of earshot—she thought—of anyone at the school. His mum wanted to warn Wills about an upcoming TV interview she'd taped that was just about to air. This was the first time (though Charles would follow suit) that Diana spoke on the record for herself, instead of simply endorsing friends to do it for her. In the now wildly famous sit-down session that has since been broadcast around the world, Princess Diana publicly criticized Prince Charles and his family—including the queen. At least one person did witness the mother-son conference and reported, "William was clearly disturbed."

That Princess Diana didn't want Wills to be blindsided by the televised interview was one thing, but just by her participation, had she not once again fanned the flames of humiliation that Wills continues to grapple with?

Chapter Eight

Saying Their "I Don'ts"—The Divorce

$\mathcal{A}$s recently as 1992 the conventional wisdom was that divorce among royals is a last resort. While there are no constitutional laws barring it, the unwritten law is that, no matter how miserable, royals stay married. Couples may, and often do, live separate lives, but for the sake of the Crown and its history, they remain legally wed. In fact, prior to the early nineties, divorce among the ruling family occurred only once or twice every 450 years or so. (Of course, in olden days, unwanted spouses were beheaded—but that's another story.)

However, society changes, and the royals—no matter how exalted—are not immune. Divorce is on the upswing everywhere. Britain, in fact, has the highest divorce rate in Europe. Its monarchy, some would say, has led the way. In 1978 Queen Elizabeth's sister, Margaret (William's great-aunt), divorced her husband, Lord Snowden. In 1992 William's aunt Anne (Charles's sister) divorced Mark Phillips (the father of cousins Peter and Zara). The 1996 divorce of Wills's uncle Andrew from Sarah Ferguson surprised no one. (In fact, of Wills's aunts and uncles on his father's side, only one is not divorced: Prince Edward, who has yet to marry). Certainly the divorce of his own parents was pretty much a given.

William's warring parents were officially separated in December 1992, yet didn't become legally divorced until August 1996. What took so long? Many have pondered just that question, but the answer isn't difficult to deduce. For one thing, British laws forbid divorce until the unhappy couple has been separated for a period of two years. Which would've brought the fractured family to the end of 1994, the year most scribes felt divorce papers should have been filed. There was a major outcry for such a permanent move because, it was argued, what if Queen Elizabeth were to die unexpectedly? Charles would automatically ascend, and along with him the not-yet-divorced Diana. And the only thing worse than a warring prince and princess would have been a publicly warring and legally separated sovereign and queen consort.

The fact that Prince Charles and Princess Diana didn't cut ties for another two years led some to postulate that there was still an outside chance at reconciliation. As remote as that sounds, in fact, sometime in 1994 Diana did secretly meet with Queen Elizabeth and agree to a tentative reconciliation—on one condition: that Charles end his relationship with Camilla Parker-Bowles. Reportedly, the Palace agreed; the only one who didn't was Charles. There were no other attempts at patching the marriage of Prince William's parents.

In fact, what the family and their lawyers had been doing for all those years was basically working out the details, and there were massive amounts to be figured out. Some were the same as any couple about to be uncoupled would have: splitting up money, possessions, homes, and the question of child custody. Other issues were quite different, for they included matters of state, titles, and ascension to the throne. The truth is, even about such areas as money, jewels, estates, possessions, everything was more complicated because there was just so much more of it!

Plus there was the matter of public opinion, more crucial to royals than to most "mortals." Should the public "side" with Diana in matters relating to the divorce, the entire monarchy, which derives its power from the love and support of the people, could be threatened. And throughout 1994, 1995, and the early part of 1996, Diana continued to wage her campaign, currying public favor. During her now famous TV interview, she said her goal was not to become Queen of England, but "queen of people's hearts." She'd been well on her way there for quite some time.

In February 1996 Diana fired a preemptive strike, meant to manipulate the media in her favor. After meeting privately with her about-to-be-ex, she went public without his or the queen's prior knowledge. Diana issued a statement saying, in effect, that she'd "agreed" to the divorce that Charles asked for. Which immediately canceled the possibility of the palace asserting that the divorce was by "mutual consent." Diana also insisted that she and Charles had agreed that she'd continue to be involved in all decisions regarding William and Harry. And lastly, that she wasn't leaving the marriage without her title, Diana, Princess of Wales.

Although Charles and the queen were taken aback that Diana went public without their permission, they couldn't outwardly slam her. The situation had to be handled gingerly. As much as Charles's family might have wanted to simply banish Diana from their lives, they couldn't. Not only was she the mother of two heirs to their throne, but for the most part, their own subjects continued to adore her. As did the princes, Wills and Harry.

Naturally, Diana was well aware of all this and knew she could probably force the royal hand of her in-laws. She wanted a generous financial settlement from Charles, of course, but most observers agree that what Diana wanted most was to remain an important influence in the lives of her sons. To put it bluntly: She didn't want the boys taken away from her after the divorce. It was not an unreasonable fear. According to British law, the Palace has the right to do just that: to assume custody of its heirs.

"There's nothing Diana can do," asserts Ingrid Seward, editor of *Majesty* magazine. "The boys belong to the royal family, not to her."

While most people would empathize with a mother's plight, more jaded types saw it as Diana's only ace in the hole in her war with Charles's family. If she retained at least partial custody, by default, she'd remain in a high profile position within the country. Which is exactly what she wanted. In other words, some people felt Diana was using Wills and Harry only as pawns in her battle to maintain the power and prestige she'd become accustomed to.

The official end to the marriage of Prince William's parents came on August 28, 1996, at precisely 10:27 A.M. in a clerk's office in London. Neither Princess Diana nor Prince Charles was present. After informing the boys, Diana retreated to her apartments at Kensington Palace; Charles to his beloved Balmoral estate. The details of the divorce were made public that day; the fallout continues to this day.

In the end Diana lost many of her statusy perks: chauffeurs, bodyguards, ladies-in-waiting were removed. Because she was no longer in line to be queen, Diana had to give up part of her title. While she continues to be known as Diana, Princess of Wales, she can no longer go by "HRH" (Her Royal Highness). According to tradition, that means commoners are no longer required to bow or curtsy in her presence: bizarrely enough, it could mean she will have to curtsy to her own sons one day! As the mother of the future king, however, Diana stays a member of the royal family, and may continue to travel on the Royal Squadron and Royal Train. In official photo ops she can stand next to her sons and not be banished to the background.

In more material matters, Diana reportedly walked away with a huge financial settlement (rumored to be in the $23 million range); which should help with her haute couture expenses, now that she can no longer charge them to the Palace. Diana kept her thirty-room apartment at Kensington Palace, rent free, as well as all the jewelry she amassed during her fifteen-year marriage.

In the most important area of her relationship to William and Harry, Diana appears to have emerged victorious—the young princes will continue to split their time evenly between their parents, which means Diana will continue to exert as much influence as she can over the future monarch.

It's assumed that both William and Harry are getting counseling at their respective schools, but publicly, of course, neither has commented on how they've been personally affected by the divorce. Which hasn't stopped others: Most observers feel that the boys' devotion to Diana was a major factor in the custody settlement. The Palace, it has been written, didn't want to treat Diana harshly, in case it should annoy their future king, who is quite devoted to his mum.

Some say, in fact, that Diana's real goal in the divorce proceedings was to be sure Charles never makes it to king: that William bypasses his dad.

Whether or not that ever comes to pass, perhaps the biggest upshot of their divorce was that the focus of Britain's attention fell ever more squarely on the slim shoulders of William. And that, of course, brings ever more attention, whether he likes it or not, to the world's most famous fifteen-year-old.

Chapter Nine

Up Close and Personal

Prince William doesn't give interviews to magazines or newspapers; he certainly doesn't go on chat shows. His friends and family don't dish about him; schoolmates face expulsion if they're found talking to the media. So how do William's curious fans find out what he's really like? Well, in spite of the "ban," people do, of course, talk—for just as a newspaper editor predicted, the eyes of the world are very much on the teen who will be king; everyone's interested in finding out what he's really like. And in spite of the pleas of his family to leave Wills alone, journalists with hidden microphones and photographers with telephoto lenses continue to provide a steady stream of photos and information. In fact, an unspoken compromise seems to have been reached between the press and the Palace: While William is on the grounds of Eton, he's pretty much given his space and left alone. However, once off the grounds, the young prince is fair game. Happily for his Wills-hungry fans, the future king has been stepping out more and more lately; friends, associates, and insiders have been talking more. Thus, a fairly complete picture of Prince William of Wales is starting to emerge.

What Wills Is Really Like

When he was little, Prince William was most often characterized as mischievous, bossy, and temperamental. No one's saying that about the future king anymore. At fifteen, William Windsor has changed a lot. These days he's a fascinating combination of wary and watchful, yet relaxed and cheerful; steely and self-confident, yet sensitive and shy; a typical teenager, yet poised beyond his years. In fact, what many observe about William is that after all the public family strife he's endured, he seems to have inherited the *best* qualities of each of his parents.

In his book, *The Decline and Fall of the House of Windsor,* Donald Spotto describes Prince William as "reserved and serious, a cautious and introverted boy who has grown wary of all the publicity. Conscious of his position and his future, he is becoming a dignified, somewhat stern teenager; his eyes often have a premature, prescient sadness." One of Wills's uncles asserts that his nephew is "a very self-possessed, intelligent, and mature boy, quite formal and stiff, sounding older than his years when he answers the phone."

Prince William does approach all new situations with a wary eye, as if always on the lookout for who's out to get him. It's hardly paranoia: People really *are* out to "sell" stories about him. So, in addition to that tracking device, Wills has learned to wear a protective emotional shell at all times. He rarely lets his guard down long enough to speak candidly and certainly tries to avoid embarrassing situations. "He's developed an emotional arsenal to survive his singular fate" is how one observer put it. More likely, he's just developed a thick skin; a handy tool when people are always aiming to take potshots at you.

Although William is quiet and might seem stuffy or uptight, it would be wrong to characterize him as cold—he's far from that. In fact, Wills is extremely sensitive, more so than he'd probably like to let on. A friend tattles, "William is a sensitive soul, and things plainly bother him." Chief among those things, no doubt, is his parents' messy divorce. Like many children of divorce, William not only feels rotten, he feels responsible. Of course, his parents' situation had nothing at all to do with him, but according to insiders, "he has taken on some of the burden of guilt of his parents' separation."

If William has developed a protective shell, he's also developed a protective side, especially when it comes to his brother, Harry, or his mother, Diana.

Wills has been helping Harry acclimate to his own royal responsibilities and showing him the ropes at school, too. It's a safe bet no one will taunt Harry when the thirteen-year-old enters Eton—they'd have to duke it out with his six-foot-tall and muscular big brother!

Ever since he was little, William has been his mother's chief comforter. According to one widely repeated story, when Di locked herself in the bathroom after a fight with Charles, Wills pushed tissues under the door, with a note saying, "I hate to see you sad." Soon after that incident Wills reportedly said, "I want to be a policeman so I can look after my mother." Since the divorce, Prince William sees himself more than ever as his mother's protector.

His mum has said, "That child is a deep thinker," and there's no question Wills has a shy, reflective, and somber side. But looks can be deceiving, and Wills isn't really bashful. Once you get to know him, it's clear that he's very sociable, cheerful, and charming as well. Like lots of boys his age, Wills loves nothing more than going out and having fun.

Fun and Games

Just how does a future heir to the throne kick out the jams and have fun? In most ways, not very differently from a lot of teenagers around the world. For in spite of his life-in-a-fishbowl existence, Prince William is trying hard—and in a lot of ways, really succeeding—at being normal, or some approximation thereof. He has lots of interests that keep him very active.

Wills has always been a major sports buff, both as a spectator and a participant. Aside from soccer, water polo, and sculling at school, he's also into tennis and plays as often as he can. Along with his mother and brother, William is a member of the exclusive Harbor Club in Chelsea, London, where he often goes for a game of singles or doubles.

Rugby, very popular in Europe, though not in the USA, is another favorite of William's. He's not on his school team, but he did get to play—just for fun—with lessons in catching, passing, and punting from the pros. Not too long ago William and Harry spent an afternoon kicking the ball around with members of England's national rugby team on their home field—which is kind of like getting to go one-on-one with Michael Jordan and members of the Chicago Bulls on their home court. In other words, for fans of the sport, it doesn't get any cooler than that.

Hockey, soccer, and swimming are also on his list of sports favorites and, of course, skiing, which he's been doing since he was very small. Wills has enjoyed the slopes of the most glamorous ski resorts the world over.

Of all the places he's visited, however, one stands out as his favorite. It's neither exotic nor exclusive; in fact, it's the number-one vacation destination for most Americans and one that many of William's fans share his enthusiasm for. That would be Disney World, in Orlando, Florida, frequently advertised as "the happiest place on earth." While Wills hasn't said if he agrees with that description, clearly he does find it magical.

Favorite attractions include the Star Wars space ride, the Indiana Jones show, the Beauty and the Beast characters, and all the water-slide rides. Don't bother checking the line to see if perhaps Wills or Harry is behind you in it, though. Not only don't the princes ever have to stand on line, they don't exactly stroll the Disney grounds at all. Instead, they're whisked through underground tunnels between one attraction and the next. Then, the princes pop up at the front of the line. Before you start feeling jealous, however, think about this: William and Harry are not allowed to leave their hotel room at night. Due to security concerns and on strict orders of the queen, the boys are confined to their Disney World suite, in which they eat dinner and from which they watch the dazzling fireworks displays going on outside.

Disney World isn't Prince William's only American vacation. Wills the thrill-seeker had an awesome time last summer vacationing in Aspen, Colorado, with his mom and brother. They were guests of movie stars Goldie Hawn and Kurt Russell, at whose estate they bunked. Wills got to ride an all-terrain vehicle over a winding trail, but best of all was the white-water rafting trip down Colorado's Roaring Fork River. Apparently, the river, near frozen and dangerously swollen by recent heavy snows, didn't treat Prince William any differently than it did anyone else: The twelve-mile ride was wild and bumpy. But while Princess Diana spent the trip clutching the side of the raft, white-knuckled with fear, Wills loved every second of it. So did Harry, who squealed, "This is great! Mum, can we do it again?"

Wills rides horses, mountain bikes, and occasionally drives his father's Range Rover, but only on the grounds of their Balmoral estate in Scotland. For the most part, he is chauffeured everywhere he goes and can look forward to more time spent in the back of a limousine than behind the wheel of any car.

Like the majority of his peers, William is a rock music fan and very much up on the top groups. The British band Pulp is his favorite, and even though he could have his mom make a call and meet almost anyone he wants, he opted for writing to the band to get an autographed poster like any other fan. He got it, too. Now his musical tastes include the Spice Girls.

Ironically, Prince William's greatest passion is the only one that's landed him in hot water, at the center of what continues to be his very own controversy. That is hunting, or shooting, as it's more commonly referred to among the Windsors. Long fascinated by guns and weapons, Wills has had extensive training and become an excellent shot—just like his father and many of his friends and relatives. Even his mother, who reportedly is no longer a fan of the sport, actually shot her first stag when she was only thirteen. William and Harry have accompanied their father on the family's bird and rabbit hunts since they were very small.

So in December 1996, when Prince William bagged his own first stag, and participated in the ritual ceremony afterward of having his face daubed with the deer's blood by hunting guides, he was surprised about the outrage it caused. Now *he* was the royal in trouble, as animal rights activists came down hard on the young prince. William himself didn't counter with a public statement, but the controversy raged on just the same.

While some regard it as the slaughter of innocent animals, others regard it as sport. And still others regard it as "de rigueur" for William in particular. As one expert explained, "Hunting, shooting, and fishing are essential prerequisites for an English country gentleman. That, along with the art of public speaking and political acumen are what's expected of William." William clearly enjoys that aspect of what's expected—he even turned down a ski trip to Switzerland in favor of more hunting late last year.

What he doesn't enjoy, and he's made it perfectly clear, are his constant chaperones. Being tailed by detectives and security guards was bad enough when he was little; it's ten times worse now that he's a privacy-intense teenager. "He loathes being chaperoned at every waking minute," according to *Hello!* magazine. "He's been heard to ask, 'Why do I have to be surrounded by policemen?'" And even though he has, for the most part, outgrown the "game" of trying to hide from his handlers, Prince William is still pretty good at giving them the slip when he's determined to.

Stylin'

They say that every picture tells a story—and every picture of Prince William says that the boy knows how to dress. While he might require constant Scotland Yard protection, it's a sure bet the fashion police aren't after him. Of course, looking good *is* part of the "job," such as it is: If you know you're going to be photographed constantly, you might as well dress up. And Wills does. So well, in fact, that he was named one of *People* magazine's Best Dressed People of 1996. "He looks and dresses like a model," they trumpeted. "He makes no mistakes."

While William's budget allows purchases from the most expensive stores, a sense of style is something that can't be bought, and William seems to have inherited his from his flawlessly dressed, fashion-plate mom. No single designer or one style dominates his wardrobe; instead, he's into versatility and dons appropriate gear as the occasion calls for it. There are the bright, warm parkas for skiing at Klosters in Switzerland; designer sweatshirts, shorts, and tennis shoes for courtside anywhere. Whatever the look, Wills looks good in anything—from Benetton trendy, to baseball cap casual, to tweedy "classically collegiate" threads for more formal occasions.

Of Privileges and Pressures

"The truth is, having money helps in every situation. The price of stardom is a loss of privacy, but . . . the money that comes with that stardom makes life easier in every other way." No, Prince William didn't say that—actually, TV star Rosie O'Donnell did—and Wills isn't technically a star, but it's a good bet he understands the concept well. Being able to afford anything your heart desires is beyond most people's imaginations, but William was born into just that kind of privilege. Money is something he not only has, it's also something he doesn't have to think about very much. He'll always have it. His parents are multimillionaires, his grandmother is said to be the wealthiest woman in the world. And Prince William will someday inherit, if not all of it, more than enough.

But that doesn't automatically make him a spendthrift. In fact, he can't really touch most of his money for several more years. He recently opened up his first bank account and made a deposit of five hundred dollars. Of course, Wills doesn't need to hit the cash machine very often: Nearly everything he needs, in a material sense, is provided for him, from clothing to cars, to concert tickets, CDs, books, movies, videos, restaurant tabs, and any other item he might covet.

Money is only one aspect of William's life of privilege. If he wants to meet famous people—like Cindy Crawford—all he has to do is ask, and Mom will have her or him to tea. Because he's a Chicago Bulls fan, William appreciated the team's souvenirs his mom brought back from a recent visit to the USA—personally autographed by superstar Michael Jordan.

But if Wills doesn't have to concern himself with

the price of things, he does pay a heavy price for all his cool perks and privileges. "You *don't* get used to people looking at you all the time. It's difficult, [especially if you] haven't chosen it. I always felt I was thrown into it. I was never given the chance—or circumstances never allowed me—to say, 'Stop! I want to get out of this. This is not what I wanted!'" Okay, so Wills didn't say that either—Princess Caroline of Monaco did—but it's another sure bet he knows exactly where she's coming from. For the flip side to Wills's fantastic existence is, of course, the complete absence of any kind of privacy.

"The royal family wouldn't be royal if it were ordinary, and ordinary freedom is something they can never take for granted. It's part of the pressure under which they must expect to live," writes Phoebe Hichens, author of *The Royal Baby Book*. The price Prince William pays for all his privileges is akin to being under siege all the time. Anything he says, anything he does, can and will be used against him—or possibly in his favor, but *used* just the same—in the court of public opinion. And since public opinion is what the monarchy depends on, that court is a far more critical one than any court of law.

Beyond watching his tongue and his step, Prince William is also expected to set a good example. He's expected to be polite at all times, to initiate conversations as protocol dictates, and to know a little about a huge variety of subjects. In the future, he'll be expected to make hundreds of speeches and meet millions of people. And it won't matter if he doesn't feel like it: He will have to do it just the same.

All of which can be a pain, but it's not nearly as bad as what was expected of his forebears. History books tell us that Edward I took command of an army when he was in his early teens. Edward VI wrote more than a hundred essays in Latin before he was ten. James I did three hours of Greek every morning before breakfast. While Wills isn't expected to meet standards like those, he *is* expected to be a role model—for his generation, and for the monarchy, which, thanks to his parents, is badly in need of a positive one.

There's one other ordinary freedom missing from the life of this extraordinary teenager: the freedom to grow up to be whatever he wants to be.

Chapter Ten

Friends—and Girlfriends

There may not be a support group for future monarchs, but there are some people Prince William could probably relate to, or ask for advice, should he ever choose to. The children of President John F. Kennedy—Caroline and especially John Junior— were never out of the limelight from the day they were born, nor are they today. Chelsea Clinton knows she's got to be poised and prudent when in public, because any silly misstep will be reported on. While these are the kinds of friends and mentors Prince William could probably use, they're hardly part of his everyday life. Instead, his classmates at Eton are, as well as his royal relatives. From those ranks, Wills must choose his friends. He'd do well to choose carefully, and by this time, he knows it.

He also knows this: For all the money and power in the world, friends cannot be bought, nor should they be. The friendship of his peers is something Prince William needs more than ever, especially as his parents continue to play tug-of-war with him. William needs friends who will be there for him, friends he can count on and confide in—without fear of being betrayed—friends he can hang out with and just have fun with. But real friends are perhaps the hardest commodity for William Windsor.

Because of his unique position, it's tricky for Prince William to know why someone wants to be his friend—is it because of his status, his wealth, his destiny? William can't ever be sure why some-one has struck up a conversation—might he or she be fishing for gossip, something to sell to the tabloids? Might a seemingly friendly dude really just want to be seen with him and, by extension, feel important? How does William know if some-one sincerely likes him for *who* he is as a person or is just currying favor because of *what* he is—a prince who will be king?

Prince William has had to develop special "radar" to be able to separate the phonies from those who honestly care about him and would still want to be his friend if he weren't wealthy, privileged, or pegged to lead his country into the next millennium. By all accounts, he's done well in his choices so far.

If there are special challenges for Wills in choos-ing his friends, there are just as many in being his friend. For one thing, potential pals must pass muster with William's relatives in Buckingham Palace. While his parents and the Palace don't necessarily interview every one of William's friends, if they did disapprove of someone, chances are that person would be out of William's life, and quickly. Being his friend, too, involves the occasional bit of subterfuge; protecting William from the ever-present stalkerazzi, or fending off too-aggressive admirers. On more than one occasion William's friends have formed a human barrier between the prince and the prying paparazzi.

If his friends have it hard, William's girlfriends— make that, potential girlfriends—face even more unique challenges. Which hasn't discouraged thousands of smitten kittens from lining up, ready to take on whatever that may entail. For Prince William, neither movie star, rocker, nor sports star, has become one of the most sought-after teen idols in the world, the swoon-worthy crush object of an entire generation.

A columnist opines, "Girls go after him because he's handsome, kind, funny, and because he's pretty on his pedestal, a glittery target." "Prince William might not be a pop star," concurs *Smash Hits* magazine's Leesa Daniels. "But he is probably the most famous teenager in the world." As such, he's been voted Britain's Number One teen idol and "Most Handsome Royal." Pinups and posters of the prince proliferate in teen magazines; as do fawning, exclamation-filled articles. Cutesy I LOVE WILLIE stickers bearing his image are affixed to the note-books of schoolgirls all over Europe. The first time *Smash Hits* magazine printed a princely pinup—not that William posed for one, of course; the shot had been taken on the Queen Mum's birthday and sold to the magazine—sales went through the roof. Any tidbit, factoid, gossip item, or rumor regarding the teenage prince is hungrily scooped up by his adoring fans. In 1995 he received one Valentine's Day card—from his mum. The following year it was fifty-four; this year it has increased tenfold.

What is it about Britain's royal heir that turns girls to mush? Though looks aren't everything, few would disagree that great looks do a teen idol make—and snogable (kissable) Wills has been declared "mad cute" by his legion of fans.

Nearly six feet tall, blue-eyed, blond, and broad-shouldered, he'd be popular with the opposite sex whether he was a prince or the Baldwin next door. Of course, the fact that he *is* royalty doesn't hurt. William is wealthy, he's famous, and any way you look at it, *he's* looking at a pretty awesome future. One British teen magazine printed a list of the top ten reasons Wills is so cool, or "fanciable." Among them: He's loaded (rich); he likes (the rock group) Pulp; he knows how to partee!; he wears trainers (sneakers) instead of sensible shoes; he's not scared of going on scary theme park rides; and he's an all-round, dead normal, diamond geezer (he's down to earth and really, really cute).

But there are other reasons girls all over the world wish to meet and hook up with William. His popularity stems not only from his hunky looks, but also from his personality. Based on what's been printed or just gossiped about William, he seems to possess all the other characteristics teenage girls rate as important. Wills seems sweet, sensitive, shy, yet noble, strong, and funny—not to mention someone who would appreciate a loyal girlfriend as much as he does real friends.

William is also someone teenage girls can relate to. One columnist put it this way: "He's a winning combination of ordinary and extraordinary. He has a look of remoteness and tangibility; he's simultaneously unique and regular."

A teen magazine editor further explained, "Girls see him as a regular boy growing up in Britain. He's the same age, or close to it, as most of his adoring fans, and shares many of their interests, including rock music, dancing, sports, movies, hip fashion, and amusement parks." It isn't hard to imagine what a date with William might include: dinner at a trendy restaurant, dancing at a hot night spot, maybe a private screening of a new movie.

While Wills hasn't spoken up publicly, he has made it known that he isn't very comfortable with his new teen idol status. Not that he isn't flattered by his popularity, he's just embarrassed by it. "He cringes at things like the *Smash Hits* poster," reveals *Daily Mail* correspondent Richard Kay, a friend of Princess Diana's. "He doesn't revel in the attention." That modesty, of course, only adds to his shy-guy appeal.

"This is the first time a member of the royal

family has been popular with teenagers," asserted the editor of *Live & Kicking* magazine. Wrong. Unbeknownst to him, and probably even to Wills, strangely enough, that honor goes to his father (!), who many years ago was featured in the pages of America's top teen magazine, *16*. Of course, Prince Charles wasn't nearly as good-looking, and therefore not quite as popular as his son. Yet, as a famous teenager of his day, he and his sister, Princess Anne, were reported on regularly.

Naturally, William has never been interviewed about exactly what type of girls he might like, but his actions make it clear that he is very interested in the opposite sex. Britain's premier crush-object has had crushes on *Baywatch* babe Pamela Lee, whose pinup was reportedly inside his locker at school, and of course, he's had supermodel Cindy Crawford to tea.

Prince William doesn't have a girlfriend, but he does lead an active social life. In spite of his natural shyness and necessary wariness, he goes out frequently, to parties, dances, mixers, and tony teenage balls. Of course, wherever he goes, the media spotlight follows. William attended his first teen dance on October 23, 1995. It was the La Fiesta ball, held at the Hammersmith Palais nightclub and was not open to the public. Invited guests, who paid thirty-five dollars a ticket to get in, were limited to one thousand private-school students. Wills attended with his friends from school—and two detectives from Scotland Yard. The extra protection turned out to be useful, as girl after girl approached the shy young prince, not only to ask for a dance, but to "steal" a kiss. To their collective chagrin, and to William's credit, he didn't acquiesce to any of those requests. For one thing, he was probably too stunned. As an eyewitness later admitted, "I think he was shocked when [girls] asked, 'Would you like to snog (make out) with me?'" For another, he knew very well the consequences of such a kiss: headline news. As he later told his mom, "Lots of girls tried to kiss me, but I didn't do anything, because the cameras were everywhere."

Wills wasn't being paranoid. Not only were the telephoto lenses of the world trained on that nightclub, so were telephone lines, open and waiting for snatches of gossip. One publication, *The Sun,* even set up a hotline phone number, so any girl who did "snatch a smacker" (snag a princely lip-lock) could report it immediately. Later, however, when officials representing the queen complained about the privacy-invading set-up tactic, the publication agreed not to quote any tattletales.

With or without any stolen smooches, William had a great time at his first dance. He bounced on an inflatable castle and threw himself into the crowd, sliding through soapy foam that covered the dance floor. He laughed, danced—apparently, he's "quite a good mover"—frolicked with his friends, and even got in line like everyone else to get a drink of bottled water.

Prince William's social life isn't restricted to dances or parties. He actually has been out on a few dates, mostly the set-up kind, however, with sisters of his friends. Not that any has been particularly romantic. How could they be, with bodyguards trailing not far behind?

The Ladies-in-Waiting

What would it take to snag the prince's eye? It would seem that those lucky lasses of privilege, in whose circles Wills already runs, do have a head start. In other words, he's more likely to meet—at this stage of his life anyway—adolescent aristocrats, girls who attend private schools, who go to the types of parties and dances he goes to, who are either wealthy, famous or, better yet, titled in their own right. Rumors even had him trading love notes with Lady Lucy Gordon, the seventeen-year-old daughter of a Scottish earl, but they were untrue. Further, those false rumors embarrassed and shocked him.

Another romantic rumor had at least a shred of truth to it—at least the girl it was centered on had met him. Her name is Alex Miller, she's fifteen, and her encounter with Prince William was quite sweet. Alex, neither titled nor privileged, was simply standing outside the church near Sandringham when William was there with his family. She handed him a bouquet of flowers, along with a note saying she felt he deserved the best in life. While the two haven't gone out yet, it has been reported that Prince William was quite touched by the simple, heartfelt gesture.

Naturally, newspapers pounced on Alex, for the truth is that *any* potential girlfriend of Prince William's will be scrutinized, even picked apart by the press. "Is she worthy," would be the underlying question, "of being our queen someday?" Prince Charles, at William's age, used to complain that he could not go on a date without the entire nation analyzing his choice, from the perspective of possible future queenship. Clearly, some things haven't changed all that much.

William's potential girlfriends will also come under the scrutiny of his family: specifically the branch currently occupying Buckingham Palace. And if a particular young lady did not measure up in some way—or wasn't considered suitable for the future king—chances are he would be strongly discouraged from seeing her. As one expert put it, "He can go out with girls of his own choosing, but they'll obviously be from a suitable background—they'll be the only girls he's allowed to meet."

While William really might be restricted for now, that doesn't mean he'll always be. It also doesn't mean Wills wouldn't eventually fall for someone outside his social circle. If he's learned anything in his complicated life, it's that all the money, privilege, and titles in the world don't guarantee happiness. To find Ms. Right—or Lady Right—he may very well assert his independence and look outside his own tight-knit milieu.

Of course, no matter the background a girl comes from, the route to William's heart is the same. Prince William goes for girls who share his interests, who like to laugh and have fun just like he does, and with whom he could open up and share his feelings. The most important criteria is simply that a girl sincerely likes him for himself—not for his wealth, fame, pedigreed family, or future. Wills is definitely on guard for girls who only want to go out with him so they can talk about him later, or be seen with him to enhance their own sense of importance. Kissing and telling is the surest way out of his affections.

Along with the fantasy of dating Prince William also comes the fantasy by extension: what the future might bring should a serious relationship ensue. For the lucky lass, perhaps there would be a fairy-tale wedding and eventually a title or two: Princess of Wales and then, someday, queen consort.

A life as William's wife *would* be filled with privilege—unimaginable wealth, glamour, status, meeting the world's most famous people, going to posh places, the toniest affairs, closets filled with the most expensive clothes and, of course, being waited on by servants, butlers, valets, maids, and ladies-in-waiting.

However, as William well knows, a life by his side would also entail a few other inevitables: constant surveillance, constant criticism, and constantly being surrounded by bodyguards. For every well-meaning well-wisher there might be hundreds more critical barbs thrown his spouse's way; for every glamour shot printed in *Majesty* or *Royalty* magazine, there might be ten unflattering poses in the tabloids; for every interview actually given, there will be many more misquotes and misinterpretations of what was really said. Such is the price of fame.

In the end the girl who does marry Prince William must know that she is also marrying an institution, the British Monarchy. And as Princess Diana is finding out, her children may belong to that institution, not to her. In short, the life of Mrs. William Windsor, heir to the crown of England, would be as complicated as his life is.

Interestingly enough, besotted teenagers aren't the only ones pondering William's choice of a bride. A British historian named Linda Colley has been thinking about it, too. "Who will he find to marry him?" she asks rhetorically. "Traditionally, royal brides are deemed acceptable for their acquiescence and sense of duty." In other words, the girls who do get the monarchy's stamp of approval are usually socially inexperienced, without careers or any hint of scandal, and more dependent than independent. "Which is hard to find in today's world," acknowledges the historian.

Which leads to the question: Will William follow the pattern set so many years before him and marry someone acceptable to his family, whether he loves her or not? Or will he take a bold, independent step into the future and marry for love, whether she is "suitable" or not? Stay tuned!

Chapter Eleven

.

My Three Lives

One fallout from the divorce of Prince William's parents is that his own life has become more fragmented than ever. For the past several years he and his brother, Harry, have been bouncing between Prince Charles and Princess Diana. These days the fifteen-year-old heir to the Crown has yet another place he must also bounce to more and more frequently: the Crown itself, in the formidable form of his grandmother, Queen Elizabeth II. William's formal training for his career won't begin until he is eighteen, but his informal training is in full effect.

No doubt Queen Elizabeth is pleased that Eton College is so close to her weekend residence, Windsor Castle. The proximity makes it convenient for

Wills and his grandmother to spend time together, which they do with increasing frequency these days. It isn't just the normal desire of a grandmother to see her grandson that precipitates these visits. "The queen feels responsible for him," writes Her Majesty's biographer, Sarah Bradford. "So William often has tea with the queen by himself, Sundays at 4 P.M. A car is sent for him and they spend a couple of hours together discussing the state of 'The Firm'— the queen's term for the monarchy itself—and William's duties." At this point those include little more than the occasional walkabout, parade review, and scheduling of official photo shoots, but William is apprised of every detail, and even allowed to make some of his own decisions about them. When William and Harry were on hand for the annual V-J Day Parade last year, a photographer caught them looking at their watches with a "Is this over yet?" expression on their young faces. One assumes that during William's visits with his grandmother, she is explaining that although boredom may be an occupational hazard, he probably ought not make it so obvious.

Queen Elizabeth and Prince William also spend valuable time going over family history. Of course, that history just so happens to be the history of an entire nation. By making him privy to historical letters and papers written by past kings and prime ministers, Queen Elizabeth is very much giving Wills a sense of what his role will be, and where he fits in the picture.

Since she has the constitutional right to supervise

his upbringing, the queen no doubt feels it's within her domain to point out what she feels is conduct unbecoming—or, as is more often the case, clothing unbecoming. And she has reportedly told Prince William more than once that, in her royal opinion, jeans, sweatshirts, and baseball caps are inappropriate attire for a royal heir. She's also reportedly scolded him for ditching his bodyguards, a practice she finds downright dangerous.

Prince William also puts in "command performances" at Grandma's weekday residence, Buckingham Palace, where he not only meets with her but spends time with trusted staff members who do their part in the grooming of the future king. This added dimension to his education will doubtless only increase as the years go by. Now that Prince Charles and Princess Diana's divorce is final, most experts agree, "William will come more and more under the influence of the queen. Slowly but surely, the royal family will take over his life."

When Wills isn't in school or with his grandmother, his time remains evenly split between Dad and Mom. And the split in how he spends his time with his still-warring parents is ever deepening.

Basically, when he's with his father, Prince William's lifestyle is very much that of a titled English country gentleman. Emphasis is put on field sports, proper conservative attire, and gourmet dining, prepared in-house by a well-trained staff. In other words, there are no golden arches around Prince Charles's country estates, Balmoral in Scotland, or

Sandringham in the north of England. There are, however, broad open moors to wander around, streams for fishing, trails for hiking and horseback riding, and acres of land stocked with game birds for shooting and deer for stalking. By all accounts Wills remains an expert and enthusiastic shot.

His grandmother would no doubt approve of William's wardrobe when he's with Prince Charles. Jeans and sweatshirts give way to proper traditional tweed suits and polished shoes. As befits his station—and in preparation for his future—William's father gave him a rather unique gift for his thirteenth birthday: a valet to call his own, that is, a servant whose job it is to assist with those clothes and attend to other personal matters. William is also encouraged to behave in an "adult" manner; that is, remain aloof and reserved as opposed to demonstrative and huggy. Discipline is reportedly strict.

Mealtimes are formal dress-up occasions where such fare as venison or a game bird is normal. But Prince Charles is also known for his keen interest in the environment, and growing his own organic vegetables and herbs, which are often served alongside the main meat dish. "I happen to believe that if you treat the land with love and respect . . . it will repay you in kind," Prince Charles told *Time* magazine. No doubt, he is sharing that wisdom with William.

The people William and Harry hang out with during their "dad days" remain the same folks who've played an important part in Charles's life and in the boys' for several years now. Since the divorce, Camilla Parker-Bowles is more publicly part of Charles's life, which means William, too, sees more of her. There is always speculation, in fact, that she may become his stepmother one of these days. Tiggy Legge-Bourke is more friend than nanny now, and she is often on hand at Balmoral or Sandringham. As she told London's Sunday *Times,* "I give the princes what they need—fresh air, a rifle, and a horse." Reportedly, she also gives William a shoulder to lean on at times. "She can laugh him out of a bad mood," agree royals experts.

Unsurprisingly, when William and Harry are with Diana, it's kick-back time. Everything is looser, from what they wear (designer casual) to where they eat (fast food and trendy restaurants), to how they normally act (affectionately, with hugs and kisses all around).

If they're not at home in London's Kensington Palace, William, Harry, and Diana are off to some fun-filled exotic vacation location, from the sun, sand, and surf of the Caribbean to the powdery ski slopes in Switzerland. They also hit the current movies as well as do all the mundane stuff, like doctor and dentist visits.

Just as they did when they were smaller, William and Harry sometimes go with Diana on her goodwill missions to homeless shelters and hospitals and come into contact with their country's disadvantaged people. The purpose, according to Princess Diana, is so both princes will "better understand people's emotions, insecurities, distress, hopes, and dreams."

Which of the divergent lifestyles would Wills

choose if he had his druthers? It might seem obvious that any teenager would choose to spend all his time with the fun-loving, yet socially conscious Diana— but Prince William of Wales is not just any teenager. And the choice, were he to get one, isn't as clear-cut as it looks. For along with the laughs and merriment and "normal" stuff provided by his mom also come the cameras and the unending publicity. Diana may never be queen of England, but she continues to wear the crown as the most photographed woman in the entire world. When William is with her, any shot at privacy is either slim or none.

On the other hand the more formal, and stuffy, atmosphere provided by his father brings with it a respite from the media frenzy. The cameras don't tail Prince Charles as they do Princess Diana. By extension, when Wills is with Charles, he's pretty much out of the prying public eye: a situation he clearly appreciates. As one photographer has observed, "William is happier with Charles. Physically, you notice the difference—he is more relaxed; it's clearly an easier relationship. But when William is with Diana, it's heads down all the time."

Clearly, William seems torn between the two. He loves and respects his father and truly enjoys the activities they share. He is devoted to his mother and, additionally, feels highly protective of her. And, apart from the glare of the spotlight, he does groove on all the cool vacations and more relaxed atmosphere. Not that William will ever have to choose between his parents, but it certainly doesn't help that they continue to be at public odds: only recently, Diana caused a controversy with disparaging remarks aimed at Tiggy Legge-Bourke, who fired off a lawsuit aimed at the princess.

Worst of all for William has to be the Christmas holidays. By tradition, he is bound to spend them with the royal family at Sandringham. Although Diana is often invited, due to the strife of recent years, she hasn't always come. It hurts William not to have his mother around that time of the year, and it hurts more knowing how terribly she misses him and Harry, and how alone she must feel without them. "It's a massive wrench for her not to be with the boys," reports a friend.

Prince William can't escape his destiny, and who knows? He just might want to embrace it someday anyway. Everything he learns being around his grandmother and with his father is crucial if he's going to carry on the proud tradition of the monarchy. And yet everything he has learned from being around his mother just may make him a more compassionate leader, certainly more in touch with the common people he will someday lead. While the Charles faction strongly believes that "Diana's influence will wane, and William will become more ensconced with the Windsors," her believers counter that "Diana doesn't want to take Wills away from the House of Windsor, she just wants to give him a different perspective."

History will tell just what the effect of that unique tug-of-princely-war will be.

Chapter Twelve

A Date with Destiny

*W*hat will the future bring for Prince William of Wales? Only two things are certain: college and kingdom. Everything in between those two events is pretty much up for grabs.

William's immediate future is easiest to predict. He'll remain at Eton for another three years. He's quite comfortable there, and continues to do well academically, socially, and athletically. Then, like many high school graduates, he'll decide which university to attend. While many offspring of the titled and the royal choose to come to the United States for their college education, it's doubtful Wills would. The queen, for one, would highly disapprove of him spending that much time out of England. More likely, he'll remain on his home turf, and attend either Trinity or Oxford, two of the most prestigious and historical universities in Great Britain.

After college graduation, less is certain. The long tradition for royal heirs is to enter the navy and put in several years of service. William's grandfather, his father, and his uncle Andrew did just that, with varying degrees of satisfaction: While Prince Philip and Prince Andrew took to the seas naturally, Prince Charles hated it. As a child, William reveled in military pomp, pageantry, and uniforms, but in recent years, he seems less gung-ho about all that regimentation. *Majesty* magazine once reported that William confided to his mother that he most definitely did *not* want to enter the navy. However, he has several years to reconsider and very well might change his mind.

What happens after a possible military stint is hazier still. After all, it's not as if Prince William will have to go out and find a job. One awaits, of course. He won't have to make a living, as a major stash is also waiting. In fact "waiting" pretty much defines the bulk of what Wills can expect to be doing: waiting for his turn at the throne, his date with destiny. He need not look further than his own father to realize that can be a very long wait indeed.

While Wills waits, he may see less and less of his mother. Princess Diana swore, after the divorce, that she wouldn't accept being "Britain's forsaken princess," but will continue as an unofficial goodwill ambassador raising money for important charities worldwide, including the Red Cross. That certainly involves a good deal of travel and high-profile appearances. There's every reason to expect Diana will remain the most photographed woman in the world. It may be true that Prince William's life will start centering more around his father, Buckingham Palace, and his royal duties, but his devotion to his mother will no doubt remain strong.

In the meantime, life as William knows it will only get more intense. He can count on even more princely perks, privileges, and indulgences, but he can also count on even closer media scrutiny. The older William gets, the more he can expect to be dissected in the press: Whatever "kid" gloves there were, due to his "kid" status, will disappear entirely as he draws closer to manhood. Any impulsive word or gesture—let alone, act—will probably land him in hot water. Even if he says nothing at all, he'll continue to be analyzed, his future the subject of endless public debate.

Naturally, as he matures, he'll be accorded more royal duties. He'll go out on goodwill tours of his own, he'll make speeches, visit hospitals, inspect the troops, and try his best to uphold the Crown with dignity and be a worthy symbol of the British monarchy, even before he steps up to the throne.

That's the subject, of course, about which there has been the most debate. Ever since his parents' bad behavior became public, and their 1992 separation, the voices of concern for the sanctity of the throne have grown louder. Though much has been smoothed over since Prince Charles and Princess Diana's divorce, there is still a large faction wondering if Prince William should indeed leapfrog ahead of his own father for the kingship.

There are many reasons for the speculation. While the British constitution does not forbid a divorced man from becoming king, the last time that happened was 1540. More problematic than Prince Charles's divorced status is the possibility that he wants to remarry. Alas, the woman he has always loved, Camilla Parker-Bowles, has many strikes against her, enough to possibly prevent Prince Charles from becoming king should he marry her.

As it stands now—and there is reason to believe this may change—there are problems on the religious front. Upon Queen Elizabeth's death, Charles automatically becomes Supreme Governor of the Church of England, one of the major political and spiritual powers in Britain. Remarriage within the church would be unpalatable to the clergy, who do not perform marriages for divorcees. While Charles could circumvent that problem by marrying in the Church of Scotland, which is less strict, that wouldn't help with the other big issue: public perception. Up until the end of 1996, surveys showed that most of the British people were dead set against the possibility of a Queen Camilla, 5 to 1. Why should Prince Charles care what others think? As experts maintain, "The monarchy depends on the public's acceptability. If Charles married Camilla before he became king, it is more than possible that the public would vehemently oppose his succession. And if public opinion is against it, he would almost have to step aside."

However, very recently, reforms have been proposed by the royal family itself that may make it easier for Prince Charles to marry Camilla and still become King Charles. The proposals are sweeping. They include a change in the laws of succession, giving firstborn daughters equal rights of ascension—in other words, girls would no longer be pushed aside by a younger brother for the right to be sovereign. The reforms also include allowing monarchs to marry Roman Catholics (which they could not do before) and, as such, remove them from the automatic position of secular head of the Anglican Church. That in and of itself would take away one giant obstacle from Charles. As for Mrs. Parker-Bowles, she also seems to be taking steps to gain public favor, by hiring a PR company to boost her image. One observer put it quite bluntly: "Charles has no intention of marrying unless he can do so without sacrificing the Crown."

Still, there are those who feel that time is his greatest enemy. Prince Charles is already forty-eight, and his mother continues to be in superior health. There is no reason to believe that she won't continue to reign for as long as another dozen years. Just recently, however, the monarchy addressed that very issue. It announced a five-year plan, ostensibly to allow Prince Charles to get back into the good graces of the British people. The year 2002, it is now predicted, is the year Queen Elizabeth will finally cede the Crown to her firstborn: She will have ruled an even fifty years. Charles himself will be fifty-three, not an unheard of age to become king. At that point Prince William officially becomes the Prince of Wales, and, at nineteen, legally of age to take charge should his dad's reign either become stalled or not happen at all.

Right now William is much more popular than his father. In spite of the controversy that surrounds his hunting hobby, he is almost universally well liked. Astoundingly, in a *Time* magazine survey of the Top Ten newsmakers of 1996, under "International Affairs," Wills was listed along with Pope John Paul II and Boutros Boutros-Ghahli, secretary-general of the United Nations. Prince Charles wasn't even mentioned.

Edward Pilkington, a journalist who covers the royals, opines, "The monarchy needs someone who is seen to be as popular as Diana—and I think [William] probably will be. And it needs someone who is prepared to change it, bring it into step with other institutions of the next century." In that sense, it could be argued that the training William received from his mother, less traditional, but much more in step with the people, will prove to be at least as valuable as his historical, steeped-in-tradition training he gets from his dad's side of the family.

In June 1996, *Time* magazine pointed out that "Wills will have a powerful role in shaping the monarchy in the coming century. He cannot afford to stumble. The burdens are enormous, but at least he is surrounded by billowing gusts of goodwill. He may be the stable leader who is so badly needed to strengthen a besieged but valuable institution."

Should that prediction prove true—that a boy who grew up mired in the instability of his parents should become the most stable of leaders—the irony would be hard to miss.

The other issue, of course, is the perception that William doesn't want to be king and has said so. According to an article in *Royalty* magazine, "Prince William has told his parents that he does not want to become king. Friends of the Princess of Wales claim that William confessed his feelings to his parents and that his father was surprised, while his mother said she would support her son in anything he chose to do."

That quote made its way to headline status around the world. What hasn't received the same publicity, however, is that Prince William was quite young when he made that statement and may very well have already reversed himself.

Indeed, the original article went on to assure worried monarchists that "both Charles and Diana are said not to be too concerned; both think it is a passing phase." It noted further, however, that if Wills did remain steadfast in his opposition to the throne, he'd still have to ascend—and then abdicate.

Should that happen, would that mean the end of the British monarchy? It's doubtful. In spite of the scandal, ill-will, and general bad behavior over the past two decades, the overwhelming majority of Brits still believe in it. After a historic public debate on the topic "Do you still want a monarchy?" held in January 1997, the votes came in overwhelmingly in support of continuing the grand historic tradition. With or without Wills, the monarchy would live on; Prince Harry, of course, is next in line.

What Does a King Do?

As king, William will occupy the ancient English throne. What exactly will his job be? What power will he wield? According to expert and author Donald Spotto, lots. There are 270 million subjects in the British Commonwealth, all of whom will call William His Majesty. Although the British constitution guarantees that the sovereign has no direct political power, its authority is formidable.

King William V will formally open all sessions of Parliament (the actual government, similar to the U.S. Senate and House of Representatives; it is led by the prime minister) and make a speech about what "my government is going to do during the coming year." William will have the right to demand consultation with any and all government leaders, and to advise and caution them as he desires. He'll have the right to invite any member of Parliament to form a government and to convene and dissolve Parliament itself. In certain circumstances he will be able to declare a state of emergency all across the country, mobilize militia or command existing armed forces: All serving members of all branches of the military swear allegiance, not to their country, but to their monarch.

More important, perhaps, he will be above the often divisive nature of politics and, instead, symbolize the unity of his country. His portrait will appear on England's currency, coins, and bills and that of many other Commonwealth countries.

Wills may pop up in tabloids and newspapers today; one day the reign of King William V will be analyzed in history textbooks. His grandmother, Queen Elizabeth II, may reign for fifty years; William could go as long, if not longer.

The story of Prince William of Wales is just beginning.

Facts at Your Fingertips

Real Full Name: William Arthur Philip Louis Windsor

Also Known As: Prince William

Will Be Known As: His Royal Highness, The Prince of Wales (when his father becomes king)

Will Be Hailed As: His Majesty King William V

Born At: St. Mary's Hospital, Paddington, London

Birthday: June 21, 1982

Sign: Gemini

Hair and Eye Color: Blond, blue

Height: 5 feet, 10 inches tall

Parents: His Royal Highness Prince Charles of Wales and Princess Diana

Grandparents: Her Majesty Queen Elizabeth II; The Duke of Edinborough, Philip Mountbatten; plus (on his mom's side) Frances Shand Kydd and the late Earl of Spencer

Great-grandparents: The Queen Mother, Elizabeth Bowes-Lyon (affectionately referred to as the Queen Mum) and the late King George VI

Brother: Prince Henry Charles Albert David Windsor, usually called Harry, born September 15, 1984

Other Famous Kin: His uncles, Prince Andrew and Prince Edward; his aunts, Sarah Ferguson and Princess Anne; cousins Peter and Zara Phillips, plus Princesses Beatrice and Eugenie

Will His Relatives Continue to Embarrass Him? Looks that way. Most of William's relatives have been divorced, publicly and messily.

Pets: A Labrador puppy named Widgeon, named for a type of wild duck

Homes: Kensington Palace (where Mom lives); plus the estates Highgrove and Balmoral (where Dad is usually found). Also, Wills is welcome at Grandma's places: Buckingham Palace, Windsor Castle, the estate at Sandringham.

Schools: Mrs. Mynors' Nursery School, 1985–1987; Wetherby School, 1987–1990; Ludgrove School, 1990–1995; Eton College, 1995–2000 (estimated)

Favorites

Food: Burgers, fries, pizza, pasta, chocolates; but also his dad's homegrown veggies, free-range eggs, and venison

Drink: Coke

Bands: Pulp, Spice Girls

Sports: Skiing, tennis, soccer, hockey, swimming, fishing, hunting

For Fun: Video games

Vacation: Disney World

Crushes: Pamela Lee, Cindy Crawford

Hidden Talent: William is quite an accomplished artist. His pencil sketch of a stone house was featured at Eton's art show.

Biggest Achievement: Keeping his sanity while his parents' marriage fell apart

Biggest Mistake: Tends to take himself a bit too seriously

Did You Know?

Historical Tidbit: An eldest son of an eldest son has not ascended to the British throne in two hundred years, since George III succeeded George II.

Little Known Factoid: It is a rule that when the queen and members of her family travel, separate lavatories are provided for their use only.

The Write Stuff: Wills is left-handed.

Moms says: "He's a deep thinker."

Dad says: "I feel sorry for him."

The Royal Line from Queen Victoria to the Present

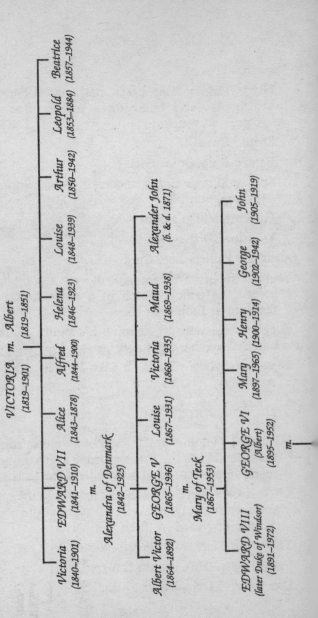

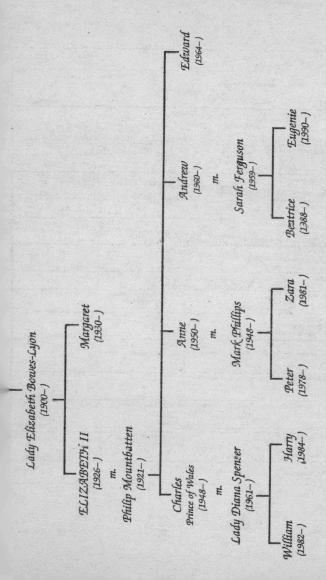

| NHS Number | LSBSS 115 | **BIRTH** | Entry No. | **115** |

| Registration district | Westminster | Administrative area |
| Sub-district | Westminster | City of Westminster |

1. Date and place of birth
CHILD
Twenty first June 1982
St Mary Hospital Praed Street Westminster

2. Name and surname His Royal Highness Prince William Arthur Philip Louis

3. Sex Male

FATHER
4. Name and surname His Royal Highness Prince Charles Philip Arthur George Prince of Wales

5. Place of birth Westminster

6. Occupation Prince of the United Kingdom

MOTHER
7. Name and surname Her Royal Highness The Princess of Wales

8. Place of birth Sandringham Norfolk

9.(a) Maiden surname SPENCER

(b) Surname at marriage if different from maiden surname —

10. Usual address (if different from place of child's birth) Highgrove Near Tetbury Gloucestershire

INFORMANT
11. Name and surname (if not the mother or father)

12. Qualification Father

13. Usual address (if different from that in 10 above) —

14. I certify that the particulars entered above are true to the best of my knowledge and belief
Charles .... Signature of informant

15. Date of registration Nineteenth July 1982

16. Signature of registrar Joan V. Dele Registrar

17. Name given after registration, and surname

About the Author

Randi Reisfeld is a best-selling author of several titles in the *Clueless* series: *An American Betty in Paris; Cher's Furiously Fit Workout; Cher Goes Enviro-Mental;* and *Too Hottie to Handle*. She has written more than a dozen celebrity biographies including *The Kerrigan Courage: Nancy's Story* and *This Is the Sound: Today's Top Alternative Bands*. Among her recent releases is *Who's Your Fave Rave? 40 Years of 16 Magazine*. She lives in the New York area with her family and the family dog, Peabo.

Real Life Stories
from Archway Paperbacks

CELEBRITY BIOGRAPHIES
◆ Melrose Place:
Meet the Stars of the Hottest New TV Show

◆ Prince William: The Boy Who Will Be King

◆ Joey Lawrence
by Randi Reisfeld

◆ Jonathan Taylor Thomas: Totally JTT!
by Michael-Anne Johns

◆ Will Power! A Biography of Will Smith
by Jan Berenson

SPORTS BIOGRAPHIES
◆ Michael Jordan: A Biography

◆ Shaquille O'Neal: A Biography

◆ Grant Hill: A Biography
by Bill Gutman

INSPIRING AUTOBIOGRAPHIES
◆ Warriors Don't Cry: A Searing Memoir of the
Battle to Integrate Little Rock's Central High
by Melba Pattillo Beals

◆ To the Stars: The Autobiography of George
Takei, Star Trek's Mr. Sulu
by George Takei

Archway paperbacks
Published by Pocket Books
1340

Don't Miss a Single Play!

Archway Paperbacks Brings You the Greatest
Games, Teams and Players in Sports!

By

Bill Gutman

☆NBA® High-Flyers   88739-4/$3.50
☆Football Super Teams   74098-9/$2.95
☆Bo Jackson: A Biography   73363-X/$2.99
☆Michael Jordan: A Biography (revised)   51972-7/$3.99
☆Baseball Super Teams   74099-7/$2.99
☆Great Sports Upsets 2   78154-5/$2.99
☆Great Quarterbacks of the NFL   79244-X/$3.50
☆Shaquille O'Neal   88088-8/$3.99
☆Grant Hill: A Biography   88738-6/$3.99

An Archway Paperback
Published by Pocket Books

Simon & Schuster Mail Order
200 Old Tappan Rd., Old Tappan, N.J. 07675
Please send me the books I have checked above. I am enclosing $_____ (please add $0.75 to cover the postage and handling for each order. Please add appropriate sales tax). Send check or money order–no cash or C.O.D.'s please. Allow up to six weeks for delivery. For purchase over $10.00 you may use VISA: card number, expiration date and customer signature must be included.

POCKET
B O O K S

Name _____

Address _____

City _____   State/Zip _____

VISA Card # _____   Exp. Date _____

Signature _____

630-07

Let's Talk About ME!

The teenage girl's interactive handbook for the 21st century.

Get the CD-ROM that YM Magazine says "you should definitely check out. It's *totally* interactive."

Including:

An Ultimate Closet
A Password Protected Diary
Quizzes & Horoscopes
A Virtual Hair Salon

This is NOT your brother's software!

Order it today!

Just $29.95

(plus shipping & handling)

Call toll free 1-888-793-9972

promo key 440115

1306